Death in a Desert Garden

Death in a Desert Garden

A Bea Rivers Mystery

Marty Eberhardt

**Artemesia
Publishing**

ISBN: 9781951122225 (paperback) / 9781951122300 (ebook)
LCCN: 2021938504
Copyright © 2021 by Marty Eberhardt
Cover illustration copyright © 2021 by Bill Singleton

Printed in the United States of America.

Artemesia Publishing
9 Mockingbird Hill Rd
Tijeras, New Mexico 87059
info@artemesiapublishing.com
www.apbooks.net

First Edition

Advance Praise for *Death in a Desert Garden*

Take a peaceful desert botanical garden, add a small, dedicated staff, and a quirky board of directors with decades of hidden simmering resentments. When a partially severed tree limb kills the widow of the founder of the garden, everyone is a suspect. The lush descriptions of the plants and the ecological considerations involved in running a desert garden are the canvas on which the investigation unfolds. You'll keep turning the pages until the totally unexpected conclusion.

> Carolyn Niethammer, award-winning author of eleven books on the food and people of the Southwest.

Combining a determined sleuth who skillfully navigates all levels of Tucson society, with such a vivid sense of the Southwest you feel the blistering summer heat from the page and see the unexpected beauty of the desert, with a mystery that will keep you guessing until the final pages — makes Marty Eberhardt's Death in a Desert Garden a first-rate addition to the ranks of debut mystery novels. Brava!"

> Kris Neri, NM-AZ Book Award-winning author of *Hopscotch Life*

Marty Eberhardt expertly draws the reader into the beauty and danger of the desert, weaving elements of the traditional mystery into the story along the way. The result is a great read!

> Marty Wingate, author of the First Edition Library mysteries and the Potting Shed mysteries

To Phil, with love

CHAPTER ONE

Bea Rivers was late to work. A gust of burning wind hit her like an enormous blow-drier, but she was cheered by this assault. The summer rains might not be far behind. She'd never liked June in Tucson—everyone was testy, checking the sky multiple times a day for the anvil-shaped clouds that meant the monsoons were coming.

Angus McFee greeted her with, "What do you think? Another week? Ten days before we get wet?" He was fixing a clogged drip irrigation emitter in the entrance garden, a collection of low-water-use shrubs and trees from around the world. His comforting presence was one of the reasons she was glad she'd quit her teaching job last summer to join the staff of Shandley Gardens. Angus had become a sort of grandfather figure for her kids, who ran to find him whenever they came to her office. He was gray-haired and gray-bearded under his broad-brimmed straw hat, held on against the wind by a drawstring under his throat. His skinny legs were as tan as the rest of him; shorts and long-sleeved denim shirts were his summer uniform. When he looked at her, as he did now, she noticed all the smile lines by his blue eyes.

As the volunteer and education coordinator, Bea got to do every day what she'd been able to enjoy on once-a-year outdoor field trips as a teacher. Of course, she'd taken pay and benefits cuts, and yes, she had to work some evenings and weekends, and finding childcare at those times was tough. But she'd traded a double-wide classroom trailer for fifteen acres of gardens and another twenty-five of wild desert, abutting Saguaro National Park East, which stretched to the Rincon Mountains' conifer-studded slopes.

1

"Did you have trouble finding Andy's shoes again?" Angus asked.

"Am I that late? No, they were in his closet this time, not in the kitchen cupboard like last week. I just realized my tank was on empty and decided I'd better turn around and fill it up before I got all the way out here. My fault. So I guess I'd better get to work." Bea waved and disappeared behind a green-barked palo verde tree beside the wooden front door, carved with dozens of many-armed giant saguaro cacti. The palo verde's glorious yellow blooms were long spent, as were most of the flowering plants at this dry, dry, crazily hot time of year.

Bea pulled open the heavy door, where a brass plaque declared the building to be the "Administration Center" for Shandley Gardens. Angus told her he'd laughed when he had installed that plaque; it was such a grand name for Liz and Alan Shandleys' former adobe home, which was the Gardens' only building besides the tool shed. Bea wished she'd known Alan Shandley; he'd clearly been an inspired gardener. But he'd died five years ago, in 2003, long before she'd started this job, and a year before his wife Liz had turned their home into a public garden. Bea did know Liz. By all reports, she'd left the property and headed for town as soon as Alan died. This didn't surprise Bea; Liz once told her she "didn't care for gardening." Which was a strange thing for a public garden founder to say, but Liz called the gardens "Alan's thing."

The local paper had enthused, "Alan Shandley was ahead of his time. When other Tucson gardeners were trying to imitate the East Coast and Midwestern landscapes of their youth, Alan embraced the desert. Some of the plants he found from desert landscapes worldwide are now beautiful mature specimens. And his wife is turning this jewel over to the public!" Liz did seem to care about the accolades she got for making the "jewel" public. It was wonderful that she'd made her longtime home a nonprofit botanical garden, except that there wasn't quite enough money to pay the people needed to operate a fine public garden. Bea hoped they'd find some solutions to this rather crucial problem at the upcoming board-staff retreat.

Bea passed the volunteer taking admissions fees in the hallway. He had a thick novel, which he bookmarked to greet Bea on her way in. Bea had advertised the admissions job as an "opportunity for people who love to read." That should change when the Gardens started attracting more visitors.

"I'm rereading Tolstoy," said the volunteer, a former English professor at the University of Arizona. "I don't suppose I'll get interrupted much in this weather."

Bea's boss's door was open. His office had been the master bedroom, but it now sported a brass plaque that said, "Executive Director." Liz Shandley had ordered the plaque before they'd even hired an Executive Director. Underneath, with white letters engraved in green plastic, it said "Ethan Preston."

"Hey, Bea," he said as she passed by. He looked at his watch and caught her eye. But then he continued in a voice that, fortunately, showed no irritation, "Short staff meeting at three o'clock, the witching hour. Did you see we're going for a hundred and ten degrees today?"

"Yes. We've got a kid tour first thing this morning and a bus full of German tourists coming at ten-thirty, so I've got two volunteers to split that one with me. But thank goodness nobody has scheduled a tour for this afternoon. Way too hot."

"Volunteers giving tours in this heat should get combat pay. On top of their wonderful base pay." Realizing his blunder, he continued, "Of course, you should get combat pay, too, Bea. On top of your base pay—which isn't much better than what the volunteers get."

She was a little embarrassed by this olive branch, so she ignored it. "Ethan, I think we need a few more water jugs around for visitors. There are a couple more of those big orange ones in the shed."

"Good point. I'll get Angus to put them out."

Bea's office door had no plaque, which was fine with her. She was tired of coming up with fresh responses to "Rivers, that's an interesting name for someone who works in a desert garden." She settled down at her pine desk, which had been in the original house. Ethan had a modern office desk, but she was quite happy with her antique and the large floral watercolor paintings that had come with the room.

She barely had time to start in on her emails when she got a call from Dr. Bolson up in the entrance hall with Tolstoy. "Bea, there are several carloads of children arriving in the parking lot. Lord, it looks like about fifty kids and parents."

Bea dashed out of her office and nearly ran over Angus, who was still trying to make sure that the entrance garden plants were getting enough irrigation. She herded the children around the side of the building to the brick patio where tours gathered. There seemed to be twice the number of people she'd been told to expect. As she was beginning her orientation talk, a lizard darted by. "It's just like Jurassic Park!" shrieked a little girl with a dinosaur tee shirt.

"You have these in your back yard, I'll bet," Bea told them. "It's a desert spiny lizard."

A couple of the parents were standing well away from the lizards; they seemed actually afraid, unlike their kids. One mother said quietly to Bea, "Mine are more familiar with Kung Fu Panda than backyard wildlife."

Bea decided to lead them straight through the landscaped grounds, across the lawn and through the eucalyptus grove to the wild Sonoran Desert area the staff called the "back forty." After pointing out an emerald-green scarab beetle, she pulled some white webby stuff off a prickly pear cactus pad. She squeezed it between her fingers, which turned red.

"You're bleeding!" a little boy shrieked. She said no, she wasn't; this red stuff was cochineal bugs, which had been used to dye things thousands of years ago and still were. The kids all wanted to squeeze the bugs. Bea picked three "dye gatherers" to try it. Some of the parents looked like they wanted to quash this project; one in particular puckered his lips when his little girl offered him some cochineal. Another parent picked up her cell phone, after giving Bea a pointed look. Bea assured the parents that there was a hand-washing station on the way back.

The children were still full of energy as they scrambled

into their cars, although their parents looked ready for some air conditioning. As they pulled out, the German tourists pulled in. They were well equipped with walking sticks, hiking pants, and sensible wide-brimmed sun hats. They seemed most interested in photographing the giant cacti in the cactus and succulent garden—the saguaros, but also the tree cacti from Mexico—the multi-branched organ pipes, and the huge, heavy *cardones*. Nobody complained about the weather, but then it was just one day in their lives. These tourists weren't desert dwellers, be they human, plant or animal, who had to adapt to months-long blazing summers.

At 3:00 p.m. Bea headed for the staff meeting, which included Shandley's grand total of four paid employees. In addition to Angus and Bea, Javier was the third line staff, and Ethan Preston, immaculate, ultra-professional Ethan Preston was their boss. Javier was the oldest of them and by far the most experienced desert gardener. Like Angus he was gray-haired. Years in Tucson's sun had turned him dark brown and brought deep creases to his mouth and eyes.

Bea felt fortunate to have lucked into this team.

Ethan was a little late to the meeting, and Bea found herself looking at his bookshelves. They took up most of the wall space, leaving room only for a couple of enlarged photos of the boojum forest in Baja California. Ethan's horticultural and botanical library was neatly and systematically arranged. As Bea stood to pull out a book on the flora of Baja, Ethan walked in, sat behind his desk, and cleared his throat. She sat down quickly.

Her boss swallowed before starting with, "Hi, everybody. I hope you're all having a productive day. I'm going to get right to the point. I need to talk about this upcoming retreat. It's going to have to be a real come-to-Jesus meeting. You've seen the financials. Admissions revenues aren't coming in like we need. The winter and spring visitors just aren't carrying us through the hot months. And with this economic downturn, who knows what Tucson's tourism is going to do when the season starts back up in the fall." He looked around at his staff. They were nodding.

He went on, "Nobody on the board has really been willing to donate anything much, or ask for any substantial gifts, because the word is that Liz is considering a major endowment for us. Armando Ramos seems quite certain of this, although I'm not sure why." Armando Ramos wasn't Bea's favorite board member, and she didn't have much faith in his opinions.

"Well, Buffy's been generous," Bea said. It wasn't as though all the board members were waiting for Liz to fund everything.

"You're absolutely right, of course." Ethan nodded at her. "I'll get to her in a moment. As things stand now, I think we can make it another six months, and then we'll need to cut back unless things improve. My position is the least essential; we need you two, Angus and Javier, obviously, and Bea, you're coordinating volunteers that make up the equivalent of what? About four people?"

"Well, they average about three hours a week, minus a few weeks of vacation. So yeah, the fifty of them make almost four full-time people."

"We might be able to hang on to your jobs if we can step up the fundraising. And maybe Shandley can keep an executive director if a number of things fall into place."

Ethan said all this with remarkable calm, considering that he was discussing losing his job. But then, Bea had never seen Ethan ruffled. He always dressed in Oxford cloth shirts, creased khakis, loafers, and an occasional striped necktie. His short dark hair was well cut and never out of place, although she didn't detect any mousse. He was a competitive runner, she knew, and he was certainly lean. She'd heard he was about forty, not much older than she was... but he looked younger. He seemed to have it all together, except she did wonder what he *really* thought. He was always gracious to board members, even when they were less than courteous. He asked about her children, but never volunteered anything about what *he* did in the evenings or on weekends. There weren't any clues to his personal life in his office, either—no family photos, no vacation snap shots, no mementos.

She realized her boss was waiting for a reaction from his staff members about the disturbing scenario he'd just laid out.

"Liz doesn't want this place to be anything other than top notch. I can't imagine she'd accept going backwards," Angus growled. "And besides, can you see the board taking over your job and dealing with the day-to-day headaches. For free? None of them want that." Bea nodded energetically.

Ethan turned to Javier. He didn't usually volunteer opinions. He gave a one-stroke nod, and looked at his big, calloused hands. He'd done more than any of them to make Shandley Gardens "top notch." He'd been gardening on the property for thirty years. In the time between Alan Shandley's retirement and his death, he and Javier had been inseparable, putting in long days on the fifteen landscaped acres together. Angus knew them both in those days and said they'd been more of a team than employer and employee. Javier could tell stories about the history of every plant on the grounds. Angus was now nominally Javier's boss, but Angus was fully aware that Javier knew more than he did about Shandley, despite lacking Angus's Master's in Horticulture. Angus had told Bea that Javier had refused the supervisory position, saying he "just wanted to garden." It seemed to Bea that they'd worked things out well, to Shandley Gardens' advantage. Still, she sometimes wondered how Javier felt about reporting to somebody with less knowledge of the property than he had.

Ethan was talking. Bea hoped she hadn't missed anything important. "Well, the first part of the retreat is about the Events Center. As you know, we should be able to generate quite a bit of income once we build it."

"If Liz will let us build it where we need to," said Angus.

"As Bea said earlier, Buffy has been generous. You all know she's agreed to fund almost the whole thing. Thank the Lord. We're all going to walk out there with Liz and Buffy and talk about how the lawn is the perfect site." Ethan said this with more assurance than Bea thought he really felt. Maybe it was just more than she felt.

Buffy Jones was Liz Shandley's childhood friend and Liz

had recruited Buffy for the board (along with her own son, Myron Shandley) when she'd turned her home into a public garden. Since Buffy had pledged more than a million dollars for a beautiful state-of-the-art event building on the property, you'd think Liz would agree with the location that Buffy and the rest of the board favored.

"You know Liz thinks we shouldn't change any of Alan's original plantings," Javier said. They all nodded. "I wish she'd get it that our huge lawn is out-of-date. When he first put that lawn in, Tucson was a lot smaller."

"And a lot less concerned about its water supply," Bea said.

"Well, Liz cares a lot about what people think," said Angus. "And that article in the *Tucson Post* about local heavy water-users was plenty embarrassing."

"I agree," Bea said. She'd nearly choked on her toast when she read the story calling out Shandley Gardens as one of the top water users in town. Tucson was getting hotter all the time, and being careful with water was essential for multiple reasons. She turned to Javier. "You once mentioned some quote of Alan's about gardens and change, right?"

"He used to say, 'a garden is always evolving.' I tried mentioning that to Liz once, but she didn't want to hear it."

"Maybe I can find a way to mention that quote at the retreat on Sunday," said Ethan. "But at any rate, the Events Center part of the day will be the easy part."

Angus picked up the cue. "And the hard part?"

"We are going to have a good three hours to talk about the financials and how to deal with the hole in the operating budget. Give it some thought. We need everybody's brain power."

Bea realized that whatever he might say, her job was at risk, too. The board couldn't fire her; they were Ethan's bosses, and he supervised the staff. But they could revise the budget to make layoffs inevitable.

"Okay, Ethan. I'm on it," she said.

CHAPTER TWO

Bea arrived at the Gardens the next day with her children in tow. It was a bright, cloudless, scorching Saturday morning. She often worked Saturdays since this was the best time to schedule classes. Today's offering, "You're Not in Kansas Anymore, Dorothy!" would be taught by another of Bea's volunteers, Dr. Joan Madsden, a retired University of Arizona plant sciences professor and that rare species of academic who communicated beautifully with the general public.

One corner of Bea's office was stocked with crayons, books, and building materials of various kinds, including the kids' "secret stash" of objects found in the desert—rocks, feathers, dried cholla cactus joints, snakeskins, and occasional human artifacts like smooth colored glass. Lately five-year-old Jessie had wanted to add plastic bottles and cans that she found in the desert. This offended her seven-year-old brother Andy's aesthetics, but Bea pointed out that they were recycling, after all. Andy bought that, since his second-grade teacher last year had dubbed her class "The Green Team." And so, the "stash" had become an unruly pile stuffed into the closet of the Shandley bedroom that was now Bea's office.

She left the kids to it as she greeted the students, mostly retirees and others new to Tucson who had learned, painfully, that they couldn't grow their Eastern and Midwestern garden favorites in their new desert home. The class was in the Shandleys' former living room, also known as the boardroom. Today it was set up with twenty-five folding chairs and a lectern, blackboard, screen, and LCD projector cast off by the university during one of its renovations. The sketchy furnishings contrasted with the artwork on the walls. There were several woodcuts of tropical plants, and some fine oil paintings of Sonoran Desert scenes by a well-known local artist. Javier had said that Liz had taken all the "cowboy and Indians stuff" with her, but she'd left one "cowboy" painting. She and Alan were on horseback, facing each other, framed by the Rincon Mountains, two young, tall, beautiful people in full Western dress, complete with spurs and hand-tooled boots.

After Bea collected class fees from the walk-ins, she headed back to check on her children and nearly ran into Liz Shandley breezing through the hall with Buffy Jones, her buddy on the board.

Angus had told her (he'd heard it from Javier, who'd known Liz for the thirty years he'd been the Shandleys' private gardener) that they were both around eighty years old, but thanks to Tucson's finest dermatologists and hairdressers you'd never know it. Liz was nearly as blonde as she must have been in her youth. Her face was smooth, except for the distinctive cleft in her chin. But although she'd clearly done all sorts of work on her face, Bea had often noticed that Liz still had an old woman's wrinkled, liver-spotted hands. She walked with a confident stride in her simple linen shift and name-brand sandals.

Buffy was a little more bent, and she was shorter to begin with. She was almost *too* slim. Her face was noticeably smooth, but her hair made some concession to age; it was silver, professionally streaked with gold. Buffy wore Bermuda shorts, a pink polo shirt, and sneakers.

"You're here for the class?" Bea asked the two women. Class attendance would certainly be a first for them.

"Oh, no dear, we're just headed out the back door to look over the Events Center site before it heats up today. Dear Ethan has scheduled our site visit for an *abominable* time of day tomorrow, don't you think?" asked Liz. "We won't want to stand out there long."

"I suppose you're right." Bea knew that Ethan had polled

the board extensively about the best time for a four-hour retreat, and they'd chosen Sunday from one to five in the afternoon. It was definitely not Bea's first choice.

The "back door" Liz was headed towards consisted of two glass-paned French doors that led from the boardroom towards the brick patio where Bea gathered tour groups, and from there to the three-acre lawn. The class had already started, but the two women marched through it. Well, Bea thought, it *had* been Liz's house for years. Bea watched them walk through the patio and onto the lawn. It was framed to the right by Alan's rose garden, and to the left by the cactus and succulent garden, the same garden she could see out her own office window, a garden that sported not only the columnar cacti that the German tourists had loved but also masses of golden barrel cacti, a fifteen-foot-high Indian fig prickly pear hedge, a couple of boojum trees, and a whole bed of tiny South African "living stones," which looked exactly like they sounded. Tree aloes spiked through the whole area. Buffy paused for a moment before she went through the French doors and seemed to take a sweeping look at the whole area... lawn, roses, and cacti.

The class filed out a little before noon, many of them buying copies of the speaker's book—*Change Your Plant Palette!* Dr. Madsden had donated the day's decent proceeds to the Gardens. It was a successful morning, but something happened just before Bea went home that marred its smoothness.

While Bea was stacking the folding chairs after class, Buffy and Liz came back through the classroom. The two women didn't seem to notice that Bea was in the room. Buffy stopped near Bea, turned to Liz, and said, "Ethan is absolutely right on this one."

Liz just rolled her eyes and continued towards the front door. "Ethan's been wrong before, Buff," she said. Buffy noticed Bea and gave her an apologetic glance as she kept pace with her friend. Liz apparently thought Bea was one of the chairs.

Bea took her kids home, and they spent a typical Saturday

afternoon together. They did the weekly shopping and cleaning; they swam at the local pool, they made popcorn, they watched movies. She was lulled into a sense that their lives had gained some normality, after the chaos of last year's divorce. In those first few months after Pat moved out, the kids couldn't be together for ten minutes without a fight. Of course, it was their parents they were angry with, and Bea felt guilty about breaking up the family, even if Pat didn't seem to. But guilty or not, she was probably better off on her own.

The custody arrangements were even acquiring a faint regularity, after a year. Pat took them alternate Friday nights, although this weekend had been an "exception" like the dozens of exceptions those first few months. But things in Bea's personal life were improving, so maybe that pattern would continue, and the board and staff would solve the Gardens' financial problems, or at least come up with a plan they could all agree on. Bea slept better than usual that night.

* * *

"I'm glad we're still friends with the Rices," Andy announced when he got up.

"Why wouldn't we be?" asked Bea.

"Well, Mom, we're not still friends with some people we used to know," said Andy. He probably saw the guilt in her face before she forced a smile, because he continued, "But we have some new ones. Like Angus."

The best she could manage was, "You're right, Andy. Things change."

As she drove to Barb and John Rices' house, she thought about how couples always said that they'd stay friends with both of you after you divorced. This was either naïveté or a lie, depending on who said it. Bea's ex-husband had his own line of green cleaning products, and these days she never saw anybody they'd known from his work. On the other hand, she and Barb Rice had been friends since they'd both went to U.C. Santa Cruz, and Barb had been there for her solidly this whole last year of single parenthood, and the year before, too, when Bea and Pat had been going to soccer practice and out to dinner and, yes, to bed together, even though Bea had the feeling the whole time that she was living in a movie set and Pat was going home somewhere after a few takes. She'd thought the disconnect was only in her mind, but Barb had forced her to ask herself if she was denying, not dreaming.

That Sunday morning, as they sat at the table by the pool, Barb wouldn't even let her clear the table of blueberry muffin crumbs and browned omelet shards. While the kids jumped into the pool, Barb poured Bea another cup of tea and told her to "sit and watch the saguaros fruit." The white crown of flowers on the giant cacti had turned to fruits since Bea had last been at the Rices' home; the juicy things would be ready for picking soon. She'd scheduled a class about gathering saguaro fruit. Thinking about work made her realize she'd better get going or she'd be late to the retreat.

As Bea picked up her handbag and gulped her last bit of tea, Andy climbed out of the pool and said, "You work too much." Would it have felt better if he'd said it while looking her in the eye, rather than mumbling it to the pool deck? Jessie was so busy jumping in and out of the pool that she barely acknowledged her mother's departure. Bea needed to carve out some time with Andy, alone. She didn't want him to feel abandoned by both parents, and Pat's on-again, off-again attention to them had to have had an effect. She pulled the wet little boy to her for a hug. Then he did look up at her. "Have fun," she said. I really have to go to this retreat. Wish I didn't."

In the car, she shook off her worries about her kids and tried to think of a way to fix the Gardens' budget woes. Maybe there was something lurking in her subconscious. Nope, there wasn't. The Gardens could hold the most popular classes more often, and hold more events like Ethan's latest fundraising scheme, a tour of home patio gardens. But those things weren't going to generate a lot of money. The kind of money needed to pay a staff member. She hoped the board members had some good ideas.

When she pulled into the parking lot and rushed into the

building, her skirt flared in a gust of hot wind. The wind was much worse than she'd realized in the shelter of the Rices' walled patio. She was dreading making an all-too-public late entrance, but when she opened the meeting room door, she was surprised to see that there were only two people in the room. Angus was wearing his gardening clothes as usual, although he'd pulled out some very clean ones for the board retreat. He was talking with Alicia Vargas, the board president. Shandley's board of directors consisted of only five people. Alicia joined the group after the original three— the mother-and-son pair Liz and Myron Shandley, plus Liz's buddy Buffy—had decided they needed reinforcements. Setting policy and raising money for a "top-notch garden" took a lot of work, *unpaid* work, as Liz was fond of noting, and Alicia was an efficient businesswoman. She dressed the part, too. Her black linen pants fit her trim figure perfectly, her white linen shirt was not too wrinkly, and her Mexican Taxco jewelry shone with multicolored opals.

"Bea, welcome!" she said.

"I guess I'm not too late. Where is everybody?"

"They're making their way back from the lawn, slowly, I would guess, in this heat."

Alicia was probably right about this, as she was about most things. Bea was a little in awe of Alicia's competence. She ran some fine and very popular restaurants that showcased local wild foods—things like mesquite bean flour and *nopalitos,* chopped, pickled young prickly pear cactus pads.

Within thirty seconds of Alicia's statement, Ethan strode in. Shandley's Executive Director looked energized, and Bea suspected he'd had some success in convincing Liz about the Events Center site and was marshalling his energies for the budget discussion. A couple of minutes later, Dr. Ramos walked through the door that opened onto the grounds. He was the fifth board member, a botanist. After Ethan had been hired, he lobbied for some plant expertise on the board and suggested Armando Ramos, one of his jogging friends. Dr. Ramos was wearing a Hawaiian shirt, shorts, and flip-flops. "I'm not even the latest, for a change," he noted with that habit he had of twisting his mouth as if to say the joke's on *you.* Dr. Ramos—she couldn't call him Armando, although she didn't know why, she called the rest of the board members by their first names—Dr. Ramos and Ethan were as much a contrast in formality as Angus and Alicia had been when Bea first came into the room.

Buffy Jones, the esteemed donor for the Events Center, came in next, wearing pretty much what she'd had on the day before—Bermuda shorts and a polo shirt, lime green, this time, and sneakers. Her usually tidy hair was windblown today, and she looked concerned. Bea hoped the concern wasn't about her million-dollar donation. Buffy was talking to Myron, who towered over her, even with his stooped posture. He was a bit of an anomaly in this group—clearly not an outdoorsman, which was ironic, since he was the son of Alan Shandley, the Gardens' creator and a gardener extraordinaire. Myron's pallor was difficult to achieve in Tucson. He wore business clothes similar to Ethan's, but they didn't hang on him as well. "Very sorry, Alicia," he said. "Buffy and I were just checking out the night-blooming cereuses. She gives them about a week before their one-night bloom." He looked around. "Mother's not back yet?"

This was indeed the question. The other four board members were ready to start. There was widespread watch-checking: where was Liz?

"Well, we certainly can't start without Liz," said Alicia.

Bea wondered if the meeting would actually be easier without her.

They stood around and chatted for a couple of minutes—Angus gave Bea a quick rehash of the Events Center tour, which had gone well—until Ethan asked, "Bea, would you check the restrooms for Liz? Angus, could you just go out on the grounds and see if you can find her, tell her we're starting?"

Bea checked both restrooms. They were empty. When she came back into the boardroom, everyone turned to see what she'd say. She shook her head. Alicia pursed her lips, but Ethan said, "I'm sure she'll be here soon."

Five more minutes of desultory conversation followed.

"How are the roses holding up in this heat, Ethan?"

"Has anyone been to that new Indian restaurant on Swan?"

Angus came back through the French doors that led to the grounds. His skin had gone pale beneath his gardener's tan. He looked at Ethan and pointed his head towards the patio beyond the French doors. The two of them stood out there as everyone watched. Angus said something, and then Ethan stared at him like he was crazy, and they broke into a run, heading through the lawn area to the eucalyptus grove behind it.

There was an unspoken consensus and everyone in the boardroom followed them. Bea was in the lead group. She felt foolish chasing her boss but wanted to go fast enough to see where he went. That also seemed to be the reasoning of her fellow runners, Alicia Vargas and Armando Ramos. Myron and Buffy hurried along behind them. When they got to the large grove of about fifty eucalyptus trees, the branches were rustling loudly in the afternoon wind, and leaves fell as if it were a fall storm in the mountains.

Leaves were falling on something Bea had never noticed before. It took a second to realize it was a gaudy mosaic portrait of a blonde woman, about two feet wide and three feet tall. It seemed to be glued onto a wooden board, propped up on a dowel. Bea realized with a shiver that it was Liz Shandley—you couldn't mistake the cleft in her chin. She was young, with blonde hair and rosy cheeks, wearing a white cowboy hat and a white fitted western shirt with one tiny red rose on the collar. She had a bright yellow rose between her teeth. The artist either wanted her to look nasty or didn't have the skill to make her look like a reasonable person.

Bea was so transfixed by the "artwork," and so horrified that somebody had been so disrespectful to Liz—Liz was hardly her dear friend, but she didn't deserve that kind of treatment—that it took her a moment to realize that Ethan and Angus were standing somewhere else. When Buffy let out a high-pitched scream, Bea turned her head to see the two men kneeling over something. Some...*body*. It was Liz, the real Liz. The others had the same realization; there was a cacophony of short intakes of breath and a bunch of expletives from the usually proper board members.

About a hundred feet from the mosaic, father along in the eucalyptus grove, Liz was lying face up. Maybe she'd fainted at the sight of the nasty mosaic? But that was just Bea's mind trying to negate the sight of so much blood. A large branch lay beside Liz; it seemed to have broken off and hit her on the head, up near her right temple. So much blood. The branch was discolored, as if with some fungal disease.

At first Bea couldn't move a muscle, although she desperately wanted to look away. Then she was able to turn her head, but no sound came out of her mouth. This was just as well because she might have screamed even louder than Buffy had. She saw Myron, white and sweaty, rushing by her, and she turned back to see him kneel by his mother on the ground. Ethan was already kneeling there and had his hand under Liz's nose.

"She's still breathing. Here, Myron, call nine-one-one." He handed Myron his cell. Myron's fingers were shaking as they watched him punch it in. No one said anything. No one except Ethan had sprung from shock to action. Ethan half-unbuttoned and half-ripped his shirt off and used it to put pressure on the bleeding head wound.

Myron's voice was almost squeaky as he talked into Ethan's cell phone. "Yes. I will open the staff gate so the ambulance can get to the area where my mother is... lying. I'll wait for you there and get in and guide you."

Alicia rallied and assumed the Board President role. "Ethan and Myron are doing what can be done right now. I think the rest of us are in the way." She looked around at the wind-rattled branches and pulled a eucalyptus leaf out of her hair. "We should go back to the board room. We don't need anybody else getting hurt."

"Thank you, Alicia. I'll join you when the ambulance comes," said Ethan.

Bea turned around reluctantly, although she realized

Alicia was being sensible. Bea walked back with Angus because he was the one she trusted the most and wanted to be around in a crisis. She stumbled on the well-known garden path.

"Angus, I can't imagine who would create such a horrible piece of art. And what's even more confusing is why Liz would walk under the eucalyptus. The wind must be, what, twenty miles an hour right now?"

"I should have just cut the damned things down. You know I've tried to keep everybody safe from those trees!"

"I know. You even told the board that we should stay away if the weather's bad. Angus, you put up signs telling *visitors* to stay away from the eucalyptus in high winds, and Liz is hardly a visitor."

"I tried to get an arborist in to trim them last month. He broke his leg and had to cancel a lot of work. I should have just done it myself."

"Didn't you suggest that we get rid of those eukes, and Liz said no way?"

"It's ironic. In a dark way. She didn't want us to cut down mature trees, and she didn't want us to cut down trees that Alan had planted. She said they'd had good times together in the eucalyptus grove, picnics when they were young, and it was the only shade around. Her reasons seemed good enough, so I didn't push the matter. Lord knows I've been paranoid about something horrible happening to a visitor, much less a board member. But I was worried about rattlesnake bites or killer bee stings, not killer plants."

He clapped his hand over his mouth at those last words, but Bea jumped in with, "She's not dead. And Angus, it's not your fault she got hurt!"

Buffy caught up with them. She was panting lightly. "Don't beat yourself up about this, Angus. I suggested you were right about those trees, and Liz wouldn't have any of it. One of those damned branches fell on the pavement in front of me in the street, near downtown. I was only about twenty feet away. Those awful things break off all the time. Alan wouldn't have cared about them being taken out! If you're to blame, so am I."

"How about we all stop blaming ourselves and pray for my mother's speedy recovery?" Myron walked quickly by them, headed towards the locked vehicle gate. A siren was getting louder, and he broke into a trot. He unlocked the gate with his master key and the next thing they knew, the ambulance was speeding down the service road to the eucalyptus grove, presumably with Myron inside.

"That ambulance was blessedly quick," said Alicia.

Everybody got back to the boardroom and sat down, hard. The chairs were something solid in an unstable world. Then because they had to do *something*, a few started packing up their papers, but Bea didn't want to leave until Ethan came back. They heard the ambulance whiz by the building.

"I know we all want to hear what Ethan has to say," said Alicia. People were studying their fingernails and their now-moot retreat agendas, anything other than each other's eyes. Dr. Ramos pretended to read a scientific paper he'd brought with him.

"I'll go lock the vehicle gate," Angus said.

Ethan appeared about two minutes after Angus left, according to the wall clock, although it certainly felt like more than that. Bea forgot her boss would be shirtless. They watched him toss his bloody shirt into a trash can in the garden outside the French doors where they'd seen him talking frantically to Angus just a few minutes before. His hair was out of place for once, falling over one eye, and he had blood on his hands. His chest was muscled from his hours at the gym, but it was pale, and he looked less like a take-charge soldier than a swimmer who'd just been tossed by a big wave.

"What a horrible day," he said with a grimace. "Alicia, I'm sure you agree with me that this board retreat is officially over. I'll let you know how Liz is doing. Myron will update me."

"What did the EMTs say?" asked Alicia.

"They just loaded her in as quickly as possible. I know we're all pulling for her," he said.

Bea wasn't ready to leave. She couldn't make the transition to home and children just yet. Ethan and Alicia were talking in hushed voices in a corner of the room; they were in no hurry to leave, either. She threw a comment their way about needing to go to her office, and she sent Angus a look. He showed up in her office with Javier, who had been out on the grounds taking care of plants; he always worked Sundays.

"I saw the ugly picture," Javier said. They hunched towards each other, seeking solidarity. The familiar, benign world of Shandley Gardens had shifted into a place they didn't recognize.

"This really is happening to us, right? It's not some surreal movie about Shandley?" Bea asked.

Angus grimaced. "Kind of like that surreal mosaic?"

Bea shook her head to rid herself of that image, and Angus continued, "I know what you're going to say, Bea. Whoever made that mosaic didn't like her. What is *that* about? And did she walk toward the trees because she knew to look for the mosaic somehow? We all know the eucalyptus grove isn't exactly on the way between the lawn and the board room."

Bea nodded and added, "Did somebody tell her about the portrait? That kind of seems like it would be somebody at the retreat, although nobody mentioned it. Or maybe somebody told her about it before she came here, and she decided to check it out. By herself, for some reason."

They were quiet for a moment, and then Javier said, "I hope she recovers."

"I can't even go there," Bea replied.

"I can't either," said Angus. "Go be with your kids and try to have a decent weekend. I'm going to put caution tape around the perimeter of that whole eucalyptus grove so that no visitors go near it when we open for business on Tuesday. That's at least something I can do that will lessen my guilt about Liz getting hurt there."

"For God's sake, be careful," said Bea.

Ethan poked his head in the door. He'd cleaned up, combed his hair, and found another shirt. Maybe he had a stash of them in his office. "There you all are. It's time we went home. It's Sunday, after all. Javier, I know you're scheduled to work today, but go ahead and leave after you finish the essential watering. I've called the police and reported the accident and the odd mosaic. Javier, you might want to bring it in out of the wind." He started to leave and turned back. "Javier, wear your gardening gloves when you move the thing."

Ethan left, and his three staff members looked at each other.

"Okay, I'll put the damned thing in your office for the evening, Angus. Just so you both know. And of course I'll wear my gloves."

"Good, Javier. And I suggest that none of us gives much weight to that last remark of Ethan's," Angus said.

"I'll try not to," Bea said.

CHAPTER THREE

On the way to the Rices' house, Bea debated what to say. She was more than two hours early, and she didn't want to alarm Andy with tales of bleeding board members. Barb answered the door and the kids were nowhere in sight. Barb's eyebrows lifted. "What are you doing here already?"

Bea abandoned all the half-truths she'd been concocting in the car and said, "Liz Shandley got hurt. Struck by a eucalyptus branch that sheared off in the wind."

"How horrible!" Barb's eyes widened and fastened on Bea's, as if to make sure something this catastrophic could possibly be true. But Bea wasn't backing off from the awfulness of it.

"Oh, it's worse. Somebody made a nasty mosaic portrait of her. That's what she was on the way to see when she had the accident."

Barb went straight to the kitchen for a beer. "Your voice is shaky and so are your hands. Maybe this will help." She pried the lid off a strong IPA and handed it to her friend.

Bea took a long sip. "I'd better get it together."

"Having kids is helpful that way. Who knows what you would have done after the divorce if you hadn't had them."

"Oh, I might've left Tucson. Maybe taken a long road trip. Maybe gone to graduate school in biology. I've always loved plants and wanted to learn more. You know that. I guess I kind of lost myself, lost my strength during the marriage."

Barb nodded, watching her.

"I would've tried to get back to who I was before I met Pat. But you don't have those kinds of luxuries when you have little kids, as you well know."

"Yeah. What you did made sense, and it still does. You quit your teaching job and took the job at Shandley."

"Because I thought I could be outside in the desert more, learn a huge amount about plants, *and* I could bring Andy and Jessie into the Gardens sometimes. I didn't want such a separation between work and home."

"I know, Bea."

"And Barb, until today, it seemed like a smart move."

"I have to admit it's all pretty weird, but you're overreacting. It will make more sense in the morning."

Bea hoped she was right. She suspected that Barb thought it was more than "pretty weird," but she was trying to buck Bea up.

By this time, the kids had noticed she was in the house. She told them her meeting was shorter than she'd thought, so they could play Marco Polo in the pool. It turned out that Marco Polo was an undiscovered antidote for adult stress. Maybe she could make money for Shandley Gardens advertising it.

In the car, heading home, she had no trouble with the G-rated version of her day. "Mrs. Shandley had a bad fall."

"So that's why you left work early, Mom?" Andy asked.

"Yes, we couldn't have the meeting without her," Bea responded. It was one of those edited facts that she was become increasingly good at, in direct proportion to Andy's growing awareness.

After double portions of macaroni and cheese, she got the kids to bed at a reasonable hour and headed to her little room in the two-bedroom unit in the one-story apartment complex called Palo Verde Acres. The residents loved the "acres" part; it took up one block. The place was quite a comedown after the four-bedroom ranch house that she and her ex-husband Pat had shared, but there wasn't much point in bemoaning that. She turned down the covers of the double bed that had been in their former guest bedroom. It was covered by her grandmother's quilt, a pleasant geometry of pastel pinks and blues. She hadn't kept much of the artwork she and Pat had accumulated during the marriage; it felt better to look at the photographs of her father and mother, and of her kids, before she tried to sleep. She'd also kept a desert watercolor painted by an old friend, and she willed herself to meditate on that peaceful setting. Tomorrow would undoubtedly be a tough day at work. She'd have to quash the worst rumors on the volunteer grapevine and exude positivity. Inevitably, thinking about how much she needed to sleep pushed it farther away. And the day's jarring images would *not* move out of her head.

Bea got out of bed and went into the kids' bedroom. Andy, who was quite vocal about the fact that he was seven and Jessie was "only five," had crept into bed with his little sister. She looked at them there together, the skinny, worried little red-headed boy curled up around his slightly chubby, bouncy little blonde sister. His arm was flung over her in a protective, older-brother gesture. She was snuggled tight against him, and their bellies rose and fell in unison. Jessie loved everybody, but maybe Andy most of all. He was so sensitive to both his mother and his sister's moods. That had made the year before the divorce, and this year, the post-divorce year, even tougher. Andy had seen his mother's puffy eyes and tried to comfort *her,* which was the wrong way around. But it was hard to hide much in their apartment. Lately, all of them had been calmer.

Had Andy sensed his mother's worry about the incident with Liz? Was that why he'd crept into his little sister's bed?

Bea needed sleep to be a decent mother. She finally passed out three hours before the alarm rang. She dreamed of roses scattered over the ground, a trickle of dried blood linking them all.

* * *

The next day started out normally. It was over eighty degrees at 6:30 a.m., and the humidity was up, a typical pre-monsoon Tucson morning in June. Bea hadn't managed to get a brush through Andy's thatch of red hair, and she realized, as she looked at the mirror, that her own short blonde cut didn't look much better. At least her cotton dress was not too wrinkled, which was something to be grateful for. There was no time for makeup, despite the bags under her eyes. She managed to get Jessie's long blonde locks into a braid and acquiesced to her daughter's choice of clothing, which was a lavender top bedecked with unicorns and red shorts swarming with bees.

She put both kids in the back of the Corolla, double-checked the booster seat and the car seat fastenings, and turned the key. The "engine malfunction" light was on. She was just going to have to believe that she hadn't properly tightened the gas cap, because there was no time to take the thing in to the Toyota dealer. The kids' summer art and music camp did have a bus service and she might have dropped the kids at the bus stop, but they were too late for that, and far too late for a walk to the bus stop. Andy let her know that she was not being "very green, Mom." He took his Green Team responsibilities seriously, which Bea appreciated. *Most of the time.*

Bea slid into work a bit late and conducted her usual ritual when she pulled into the parking lot. She took a deep inhale and let her eyes range over the parts of Shandley Gardens that she could see from her car. This daily exercise was an expanded version of what she did at night with her desert painting. Bea didn't allow herself, for even a moment, to think about what she needed to do at work, or whether Jessie was coming down with yet another cold. She took in some of the lovely areas surrounding the former home of one of Tucson's wealthiest families. The adobe house was a modest size compared with the mega mansions of today's wealthy Tucsonans, but the Gardens were the attraction; the home beside them echoed the ground beneath them. Bea's eyes focused on the masses of barrel cacti with their golden spines and the tall, shaggy old man cacti with their white "beards." She followed the lines of the Dr. Seuss-like tree aloes back towards the native plant garden, which had been such a radical concept when Alan planted it in the 1980s. There wasn't much in bloom there at this ridiculously hot, dry, windy time of year. But there were native saguaros in that garden and beyond. The tall cacti were crowned with rings of succulent fruits. Bea's eyes followed legions of saguaros, stretching all the way into Shandley's wild desert area, up towards the national park. Miles of desert, miles of saguaros in their oh-so-human poses, reaching all the way to the foothills of the Rincon Mountains.

It was a good thing that she practiced this meditation, because when her gaze returned to the parking lot, her calm scurried off. All of the board members' cars were there—except Liz's, of course. She was surely still in the hospital. The row of cars probably meant there was an emergency meeting going on with Ethan. An emergency board meeting with the Executive Director could not be good. This might be a fine time to take some vacation days. She could take the kids to the beach in San Diego for a quick break. Swimming in chlorinated pools was their salvation in Tucson summers, but the ocean... Ethan might let her go. She could cancel her kids' places in next week's camp and get back part of her deposit... She reached for her hairbrush and tried to make herself look professional enough to talk to her boss or anybody else she ran into.

Angus met her at the front door. His eyes were dull and almost as gray as his beard today. He was pale again beneath the tan. It was the same odd color he'd had the day before, after he found Liz. Without the humor that usually lit up his face, he looked sixty, although Bea knew he was several years younger than that. He came straight to the point. "She died, Bea."

This was the possibility that Bea had been trying to block out of her mind.

"The cops are on their way."

Bea sagged against the doorjamb.

"I know, I can't believe it either," said Angus. "Lord only knows what this means for Shandley Gardens."

She caught a glimpse of two squad cars pulling up to the building, but she hurried away from them. She wasn't in her office long before her boss came in.

As usual, Ethan was perfectly dressed. He wore a freshly pressed white shirt. Well, *he* wasn't looking for missing shoes in the kitchen cabinet before work. But the day's events were ruffling even Ethan's equable disposition. He ran a hand through his hair and neglected to smooth it back down, so that he had a tuft sticking straight up over his right ear.

"Bea, Liz died of her head wounds. The police are having a look at the 'artwork' and the eucalyptus tree and that damned fallen branch, and they're probably going to want to talk to all of us. You may need to stick around all day. Thank God it's Monday." He grimaced and went out.

Easy for *him* to say. Shandley Gardens was closed on Mondays and they wouldn't have to deal with the public today, but Bea's kids were used to having a half day on Mondays, since she had to work Saturdays. She'd have to let the camp know.

She'd called the camp and nearly finished the July volunteer staffing chart when Angus knocked on the door. Two knocks, a pause, and then two knocks. Their identification code. She put the phone down and was glad she had when she got a look at Angus. He sagged into the chair across from her.

"Bea, I think they believe I killed her." She could hardly hear him.

"Oh, come on, Angus, why would you want to do that? It was an accident!"

"Maybe not. I got called in for an interview. They found some saw marks on the limb that fell on her. And Bea, it was partially sawed through, if you can believe it."

"No."

"Yeah. And climbing up in that tree would take some physical agility; not what you'd expect of a lot of the people around here... elderly board members, volunteers." Angus sighed like a tired old man who wouldn't have that kind of agility either. "*And* I was the one who found her. Plus, they didn't like it that I had already taped the whole grove off with caution tape before they got here, but heck, I was just trying to save somebody else from an accident. That's my job!"

He'd been saying all this while examining his hands. Then he looked at Bea. "Bea, you know I thought Liz was a pain in the ass, but you don't kill somebody who's a pain in the ass."

"Of course not. But who on earth would want to do that to her?"

"Well, maybe they'll decide you wanted to. I forgot to mention that you're next. They're interviewing in the volunteer room."

CHAPTER FOUR

The volunteer room had been Alan's study in the old days according to Javier. It was across the hall from the three bedrooms: Ethan's large office, and Bea and the gardeners' smaller ones. Shandley's fifty volunteers needed a place to gather, leave their coats and purses and backpacks, and record their hours. Bea hoped the police would get this solved quickly and give them back their room. For innumerable reasons.

She crossed the hall and entered the room feeling nervous, although she certainly wasn't guilty of anything. But then she was brought up short. There were two detectives at the table, and one of them was her old school friend Marcia Samuelson. Hallelujah! This was the first good thing that had happened since brunch the day before.

She and Marcia had grown up together in the Tucson Mountains on the west side of town. They used to spend all day in the desert, building forts in the arroyos with Marcia's brothers, chasing jackrabbits, catching horned lizards, and gathering prickly pear fruits for their mothers to make jelly. One day, under the shade of a big mesquite tree, they had made a pact that they would never wear lipstick or nail polish, a pact that they kept throughout junior high.

Their physical differences had belied their closeness; Bea was petite, small-boned, blonde and fair, while Marcia grew tall, dark-haired and muscular, with olive skin that tanned beautifully. As she grew older she had an imposing presence. You didn't want to mess with Marcia. The two friends went different directions in high school. Bea was a bit of a rebel and one of the "enviros" who protested

Tucson's never-ending development. Marcia was an athlete and a Student Council President. Even though they were in different cliques, they'd always stood up for each other. Bea had headed to California and U.C. Santa Cruz for college. She'd loved the green, the huge trees, and the ocean, but in the end the desert had drawn her home. Shortly after she got back, her parents swapped directions with her and moved to central California, where they'd grown up. So much for grandparents as babysitters. Marcia had stayed in town for college, going to the University of Arizona, no doubt leading all kinds of clubs.

Marcia told Bea to take a seat. She said she was in charge of the Shandley investigation, and she introduced Officer Blake, who appeared to be junior to her. He was younger than Bea, very thin, with beady eyes that seemed fixed on her face.

Marcia explained to him that she and Bea had known each other as kids. He kept his eyes on Bea. "Bea, I didn't know you took a job here," Marcia said.

"Yeah, about a year ago."

"Well, we need to know everyone's whereabouts yesterday morning and afternoon."

"You probably know we had a board retreat on Sunday. It started at one. Ethan told me I could come at two, because the first hour the board was going to tour the site for the new Events Center and they didn't need me for that. We were going to talk about our budget problems at two. I got there a little late, and lots of people were still out on the grounds."

Marcia stopped her. "Where were you before two o'clock yesterday?"

"I was at Barb and John Rice's house with my kids, Andy and Jessie. And their kids. They had us all over for brunch and swimming."

"You left the Rices' house at what time?" Officer Blake's tone seemed unnecessarily sharp.

"At quarter of two. I know because I checked my watch, and I knew I'd be late because they live about twenty minutes from here."

"We'll need their contact information," Blake said. "Now, who was in the board room when you got to work?"

"Angus was there." Marcia nodded; she had just talked to him. "He's usually on time. And Alicia, our board president, was there, talking to him. Right after I got there, the rest of them trickled in. All except Liz, I mean. Ethan told me to check the rest rooms for her and told Angus to check the grounds. She wasn't in the rest rooms, and then Angus came back and pulled Ethan out to the back patio. We knew something was wrong."

"Please tell us the order in which the others came into the board room that afternoon," said Officer Blake. He was not only sharp-toned; he was also a grammarian.

"Ethan was first. Since he set up the schedule, he needed to be on time. I remember thinking I was glad I got there before he got back. Then Myron and Buffy came in together."

"These are two of the five board members," Marcia said, consulting her notes.

"Yes. Myron's Liz's son, and Buffy's her old friend. And then Dr. Ramos. Actually, he arrived before Myron and Buffy, come to think of it. Dr. Ramos is our board botanist. I remember he said something about not being the last one to arrive, for once. Meaning that Liz was still out on the grounds. But all this happened in maybe five minutes."

"Okay, go on. You were saying that you knew something was wrong. How?" Marcia asked.

"Well, Angus looked like he was in shock. He gestured to Ethan to come outside. We all watched them through the French doors. Angus said something to Ethan, and then they both took off running."

"Towards the eucalyptus trees, correct?" Officer Blake was sitting further back in his chair, but he was still watching her closely, making notes on his laptop.

"Yes, unfortunately. They're bad in the winds. Limbs come off. And yesterday it was so hot and windy."

"Bea, it's likely that Mrs. Shandley's death was not accidental," Marcia told her.

"I heard."

"From Angus? You're close?" Marcia gave her the look Bea remembered when she was asking if she *really* wanted to let boys into their fort.

"He's a good guy."

"Is there anybody on the Shandley board or staff who's not a good person with Liz Shandley's interests at heart, in your opinion?" Marcia asked.

"I honestly can't imagine anybody planning to *murder* her."

Marcia just raised her eyebrows.

"You were closed to the public yesterday, correct?" she asked.

"Yes, that's one reason the board wanted to do the retreat on a Sunday. Normally the only person who works on Sunday is Javier."

"We haven't heard about him. Why didn't you mention him before?" Officer Blake had jumped back into the questioning.

"He wasn't part of the retreat. He didn't want to be. He told Ethan he had plenty of work to do on the grounds."

Marcia raised an eyebrow again. "So, he was out on the grounds all day?"

"Well, yes, but he's been here forever, Marcia. He was Alan Shandley's gardener. They basically created all the specialty gardens together. They were partners, or that's how Angus tells it. He knew them both before Shandley was open to the public. So, when we became a nonprofit, Liz kept Javier on as a staff member."

"What was his relationship with Liz Shandley?" Marcia asked.

Bea hesitated. "Well, he loved Alan, and she was his wife…"

"And?" Officer Blake wanted that sentence finished.

"And she treated him like a servant. I don't know how he could have liked that." The detectives exchanged a glance, and Bea said, "But he didn't dislike her enough to hurt her, Marcia!"

"Well, somebody must have disliked her a great deal.

We'll probably talk some more after I speak to the Rices." Marcia said. "Now let me confirm a couple of things. Angus and Alicia Vargas, the board president, were in the board-room when you got to work. Then everybody but Liz trickled in within about five minutes."

"Yes."

"Shandley has just five board members, including the founder's wife, Liz, her son Myron and her good friend Buffy, correct?"

"Yeah, well Liz and Myron and Buffy *were* the board. Then they hired Ethan, because they thought they needed an Executive Director, and then Ethan hired Angus, because there was too much gardening for just Javier to do. Because when Alan died, the Gardens lost a full-time gardener. Alan and Javier were brilliant at it, but Javier couldn't take care of all fifteen acres, plus some stuff on the "back forty," our twenty-five acres of desert, plus all the building mainte-nance, on his own. Then Ethan managed to get Dr. Ramos, a University of Arizona botanist, to round out the board, and also Alicia Vargas, who's in Liz and Buffy's social group, but she's different from them."

Marcia raised her eyebrows again. "How so?"

"You'll see. I won't say anything else."

"You were always polite, Bea. Okay, so that's it in terms of board and staff. Four surviving volunteer board members and four paid staff members?"

"Yes. And volunteers don't work here on Sunday. And they don't have keys."

"Ethan told us that all board and staff members have master keys that can open all of Shandley's locks. It's an interesting practice," Officer Blake said.

"Well, there aren't very many of us, and people need to get in for committee meetings and stuff."

"And everyone is trustworthy. Except perhaps not," he said, with a twist of his lips.

"Oh God, couldn't it just be some awful outside person from Liz's past?"

"Possibly. But you do have a pretty high barbed wire

fence to keep out any intruders," Marcia said.

"And the javelinas. They're a bigger problem."

"Well, wild pigs are not a subject of this investigation, Bea. The fence hasn't been cut, our investigators tell me, and there aren't any footprints leading away from the fence anywhere. And you all have keys. Including to the tool shed, which was locked, and not forced open in any way." Officer Blake had sat further back in his seat, while Marcia said all of this. His eyes were on Bea. Didn't he need to make more notes?

"Marcia, this is horrible. I guess I need to cancel all programs for the next week or so? Give the volunteers a holiday for a few days?"

"Yes, I think your boss is putting out a press release about all Liz did for the Garden, and about how she was hit by a branch in the wind. I sympathize with him—with all of you—about keeping the press out of this until we know more. I think Ethan's saying the Gardens will be closed for a couple of days to mourn Liz's death and deal with the hole it leaves in your operations. After that, all bets are off about your privacy."

"Oh, joy."

"Maybe we'll have it wrapped up by then," Marcia said.

Bea wasn't sure whether she wanted it to be "wrapped up." She certainly didn't want to think about any of her fellow staff members being a murderer, but it was almost as awful to contemplate it being one of the board members. Just a day ago she had been sitting by the pool, being waited on by her friends who said she needed a break from the stresses of work and single parenthood. She wished she could go back to what she'd considered "work stresses" just twenty-four hours ago.

After her interview, Bea joined the four surviving board members and the rest of the staff in the boardroom. A cop had been assigned there, too, maybe to report any untoward behavior. Everyone was trying to look very busy at laptops or cell phones. Dr. Ramos was reading from an actual paper document.

Officer Blake called each of them in for questioning. Bea looked up from her supposed work each time somebody came back in, along with everyone else in the room. Most interviews lasted about twenty minutes, but Myron was in longer than that. Dr. Ramos sauntered back among them with what could only be called a smirk spread across his face. Everybody else looked shaken, but guilt wasn't the only reason to look upset. Bea's hands had been visibly shaking when she'd emerged from questioning.

If Marcia was right, and Bea sincerely hoped she wasn't, then one of them had premeditated and carried out the murder of someone they all dealt with practically every day. She just couldn't believe it would be Angus, and it killed her to know he was a suspect.

Bea took what she hoped was a nonchalant look around the room. Lord, they were probably all doing this, and pretending not to. Alicia interrupted her thoughts about this by saying she'd take orders for their lunches, her treat. At least there would be *something* to look forward to. It was like being on an airplane; all of them were in that little room, pretending to be busy, avoiding talking to each other, looking forward to a meal to break the tedium. Although it was more tension than tedium, so maybe it was like being on an airplane in a storm. Except that meals wouldn't be served in a storm. She should just abandon *that* metaphor.

Alicia interrupted this aimless brain ramble by saying she'd pass out some take-out menus from the Native Delights Café. She had to get permission from their guard to get them out of her car, and he watched through the window as she walked out to the parking lot. But Alicia remained poised despite the indignity of this, thanking the officer warmly.

Bea looked forward to green chile vegetarian stew, medium-hot, with a side of goat cheese on whole wheat/mesquite loaf, and another of cholla cactus bud and sweet onion salad. Angus was partial to the Vargases' Red Hot Chicken Chiltipin Chile Stew. Chiltipines grew wild in the foothills around Tucson; Bea had read they were the ancestors of most farmed chiles.

After they had placed their orders, Bea decided she needed to break the tension. "I'm enough of a native that I have to add chiles to most mild foods, like scrambled eggs or chicken soup, but I tip my hat to anybody who can eat a whole stew full of chiltipines. Those wild little red fireballs push me to the limit." Everyone began to tell tales of their and others' chile tolerance. Despite having lived in Tucson his whole life, Myron said he preferred mild chiles, as did Buffy, who'd been in the desert "nearly as long as Myron." Dr. Ramos claimed to be a huge fan of chiltipin stew.

The meals arrived very quickly—they were ordered by the boss. But Bea noticed that Dr. Ramos's eyes had begun to water after a few bites. Angus caught her glance and his mouth curved up in a sardonic half-smile. The next time she looked over at Ramos, he was sucking surreptitiously on chunks of ice from his iced tea. He cast sidelong glances at Angus who was lapping up *his* chiltipin dish as if it were ice cream. Although Bea did detect a bit of sweat on his eyebrows.

The wind rattled the pomegranate trees facing the door. "So, when do you think the monsoons will hit?" was Ethan's opener.

"Not San Juan's Day," said Angus. The very next day was San Juan's Day, June 24. This was supposed to be the first day of the annual summer rains, but Bea couldn't remember a year when the rains had obeyed this schedule. Usually, they were later. She'd read that the Spanish explorer Coronado prayed for rain in 1540 on San Juan's Day, and it rained.

"I hope you're all coming to the San Juan's Day Celebration at Native Delights," said Alicia. Bea asked herself if she wanted to go, given everything that was happening. *Sure, why not.* It would be a good thing for her to do with her kids, and most of the people at the table with her weren't likely to get up before dawn. The ceremony started with the rising sun, and Alicia was putting the whole thing on, complete with breakfast, at her restaurant on the Tanque Verde Wash. Dr. Ramos said it was a fantastic idea, and he'd definitely be there. Buffy said she was sure it would be lovely, but she wasn't going to pledge to be there at 5:00 the next morning. "I kind of doubt I'm going to get much sleep tonight," she added.

Nobody said anything for a moment. Bea was about to continue the "When do you think it will rain?" conversation, and she could see Alicia opening her mouth to say something, but Buffy beat them both to it.

"Well, I doubt it will rain before the Fourth. We'd miss seeing 'A' Mountain catch fire," she said. Everyone in the room would understand *that* reference. The City of Tucson's annual Fourth of July fireworks display was held on a parched peak west of downtown called "A" (for Arizona) Mountain. Instead of asking if you wanted to watch the fireworks, you asked your friends if they "want to go see 'A' Mountain catch on fire." The fire trucks were always standing by and were often called into action. This was all standard Tucson monsoon season conversation.

Then Dr. Ramos launched into a detailed explanation of why the rains might be spotty this year. "Monsoons are going to get fewer and farther between," he said, turning his head towards Myron and Buffy, who both shifted in their chairs. Myron grimaced, and Alicia gave a little laugh that didn't smooth anything over.

Dr. Ramos had once told Ethan, in Bea's hearing, that his fellow board members were products of a "blessedly bygone era," which encompassed many things, she suspected, but it certainly meant they were behind the curve on climate change. Bea was watching Buffy, who had turned her head towards the French doors with a neutral expression on her face. Bea looked; there was nothing of interest out that way. Myron had now twisted his mouth in disgust. So much for board unity.

But Dr. Ramos wasn't letting up. "And climate change is all the more reason for us to site the Events Center where we've decided, getting rid of that lawn. Water conservation isn't a choice anymore." There went Ethan's earlier diplomacy. Bea was sure he hadn't brought up climate change out there; Liz usually rolled her eyes when it came up.

In that not-so-long-ago time of innocence, on Sunday

afternoon, when they were still waiting for Liz to return from the restroom or wherever they thought she was, Angus had told Bea that they'd all agreed to site the Events Center on the lawn. "Liz extracted a little more lawn out of Ethan, to preserve her dignity, but it was all good."

"All good" seemed a pretty terrible description of the state of affairs at Shandley at the moment.

"Dr. Ramos," Myron began, "as you know, my mother was not a believer in human-caused climate change. Could you do us the favor of honoring her memory by not pressing that point just now?" Much as Bea agreed with Dr. Ramos intellectually, she thought Myron was right about this.

Alicia gave Ramos a steely-eyed stare, and the rest of the group turned to see what he'd say.

For once, he backed down. "Of course."

Bea wondered, not for the first time, if Dr. Ramos had had something to do with that article about Shandley's high water use, the one that had run in the *Tucson Post.*

Then Buffy surprised her. "Well, if monsoon rainfall is going to shrink, our low-water-use gardens will be all the more essential as a teaching tool."

Was she trying to be a peacemaker? It was a good stance under the lowering boom of a murder investigation.

CHAPTER FIVE

Bea was about to tell Ethan she had to go in half an hour because Andy and Jessie would be getting off the camp bus. But Marcia summoned her to the police investigation room again. She was already calling it the "cop room" in her head. It certainly had been through a lot of changes: from Alan's study to volunteer office to cop room.

Marcia turned towards Officer Blake. Rather formally, he said, "The Rices corroborate your story and timing."

"So, Bea," Marcia said, "We could use your help in solving this crime."

I'm off the hook. Bea hadn't realized how tense she'd been until she felt her muscles release her into the chair. "Sure. What do you want to know?"

"Well, tell us what you know about these board members. You can start with Myron," Marcia said.

"Why him?"

"Well, he could have a motive. As an only child of a widow, he may inherit most of his mother's estate."

"Right." This thought had occurred to Bea, but it seemed damned uncharitable to a guy who'd just lost his mother. And he'd looked so shaken up yesterday. And today. But so had they all.

"Well, he runs Alan's real estate businesses."

"Keep going."

"You probably know that the word is he's not a good businessman. Not aggressive enough, probably. But there's enough money there to keep him very well taken care of."

"What else?" Marcia asked.

"He pretty much follows whatever his mother wanted;

on the board I mean. I kind of think he does everything he's supposed to—take on the family business, be on this board—but the rumor is that what he really loves is watercolor painting. Of indoor subjects. Flowers in vases, that sort of thing. You may have noticed he's not an outdoors person, unlike either of his parents. We're going to have a show of his work in the boardroom soon. We'll open it up to the public when we don't have meetings. Myron's never exhibited publicly, which surprises me, because he's a good artist."

"You say he's an indoor guy. I did notice his pallor." Bea thought "pallor" was putting it kindly. And even though he wore well-cut clothes, they didn't hide the fact that he was pudgy. Tall, but still pudgy.

Marcia continued, "His coloring is damned hard to achieve in Tucson. Most of us with natural pallor turn browner than he is going across the supermarket parking lot. So, Bea, anything else about Myron?"

"Well, he seems kind of old to be doing everything at his mother's behest. I mean, I think he must be in his mid-fifties?"

"Fifty-nine," said Marcia.

"There you go. Marcia, I don't know him well. Most of the board members put some distance between us and them—well, they do treat Ethan as an equal."

"Then let's come to your boss, Ethan." *How long is this going to take? I'm going to be late getting the kids.* She swallowed.

"Do you suspect Ethan?" Bea asked.

"We have a number of suspects at this time," said Officer Blake. At least he wasn't staring at her like he was at first. He was still taking notes.

"Okay, well, they hired him to turn us into a professional organization. Very few people visited the Gardens when it was just Liz, Myron, and Buffy on the board, and Javier was the only employee. If they did visit, they got lost and had questions, but there was nobody to ask. Ethan brought people to the Gardens. He got together a small professional paid staff and added some board members, and you know we're listed in all kinds of stuff as an important Tucson attraction these days. To me, he's a fair boss with a tough job."

"What was his relationship with Liz Shandley?" Blake asked.

"Well, she hired him! Although..." Bea shook her head as if to dislodge a thought.

"Although what?" Bea felt her cheeks flush when Blake asked this, tapping away at his laptop as he spoke.

"Okay. Once, when Liz didn't know I was listening, I heard her say that Ethan doesn't have the 'pedigree' she'd like. Maybe she thinks he should have gone to Harvard like her husband. Or he should have done a Master's in Garden Administration back east. I don't know what she meant, and I doubt it's relevant."

"How did Ethan feel about Liz?" Marcia asked.

"There's no way to know. He never lets a tactless thing slip from his lips. Not like Angus and me. He had to stay in Liz's good graces. He may have liked her; I have no idea. But there's also a political reason to give Liz what she wanted. She used to control the board, although now that Alicia is President, things are done by the book. But there's still no discounting Liz's importance on the board. I mean there *was* no discounting it."

Bea gave her head another shake, this time to toss out the notion that Liz was still alive.

"And there's always the donor aspect of things," she continued. "That's always a factor. Liz hadn't given much money to the Gardens, but the potential dangles out there. Marcia, I'm sorry, I meant to say the potential *was* out there. And Liz's friend Buffy is bringing a lot of money in by funding this Events Center. That's part of the plan to get us out of the hole. Ethan's very pragmatic, but I don't know what he really thinks about much of anything. Except keeping in shape. And plants. He loves plants."

"Tell me about the hole in the budget," Marcia said. *That could take a long time.* Bea crossed her legs one way and then the opposite way. She sighed.

"Is something bothering you?" Officer Blake didn't say

this in a kindly way.

"I'm going to be late to pick up my kids."

"We'll try to make this quick. So, the hole in the budget?" Marcia asked again.

"Well, we hired on all these new people—Ethan, then Angus, then me—and income just hasn't kept up with expenses. Volunteers take our admissions fees, conduct tours, staff our events, and do lots of gardening, so that saves us a ton of money, but frankly, visitors are pretty scant in the hot months. And who knows if business will really pick up when it finally cools down this fall; they're saying this financial crisis is going to make tourism tank. So, Buffy doesn't want to give us money to pay salaries or pay the utility bills, but she's happy to put her name on an Events Center. And we figure weddings could get us the money to professionalize, and have more programs, and signage, and eventually even more paid staff."

"Is everyone on board with this plan?" Marcia asked.

"Well, no. Angus doesn't like it. He calls it 'Weddings R Us.' And to be fair, weddings and bar mitzvahs and such *will* create a lot of non-gardening work for Angus and Javier."

"Angus didn't like this idea of Liz and Buffy's?" Blake leapt in with this question.

"Oh, he didn't hate the idea enough to kill anybody. It's just part of the normal disagreement you have in a place like this."

"Maybe," Marcia said. "Okay, one more question. I know you have to get back to your kids."

"Yes, thanks for saying that. Who now?"

"This Dr. Ramos." The way she said this took Bea back a few decades, when Marcia would declare, "Let's not play with *him.*"

"So, you didn't like the guy."

"I would think he dislikes cops, except he also makes no bones about disliking everybody here, except Ethan."

"And Angus and Javier. He respects their gardening knowledge. Mine, not so much."

"So why is he on this board if he has so little respect for

his peers?'

"He likes Ethan, as you mentioned. They jog together and they're both plant nerds. Ethan probably asked him to provide a botanical presence on the board. Dr. Ramos is sarcastic, but he really knows botany. He studies invasive plants, how climate change will increase them, stuff like that."

"You think everybody's 'not so bad, really.' Including that ex-husband of yours. Or you thought that once."

"Once." She was definitely not ready to go here with Marcia at the end of an excruciatingly long day. She knew that he'd had some sort of run-in with the police after they'd broken up, and maybe Marcia had been involved. She put that thought out of her mind.

"Well, Marcia, good luck. I hope you find the murderer and that it's nobody I know."

"An evil stranger, huh? Have a good rest of your day."

Bea went out into the oven that was a June afternoon in the Sonoran Desert. She'd forgotten to pull out the hot pad she kept in her purse to open burning metal door handles. She winced when she touched the driver's side door, and Angus suddenly materialized with the blue bandanna he always kept in his back pocket.

Before she put the key in the ignition, Angus said "Bea," in an urgent tone she didn't expect. She looked at him.

"Bea. Put in a good word for me with that cop you know, O.K.?" She nodded, but she wasn't used to Angus pleading with her. Her responsibilities were growing by the hour.

CHAPTER SIX

Bea ignored all speed limits. Her route was blessedly free from traffic cops, and she managed to meet the kids just as the camp bus was pulling away from the curb. Andy's look of distress turned to relief. "It was a long day, Mom," he said, as she gathered them into her arms.

This was the new reality since she no longer had summers off, as she'd had as a teacher. Andy looked up and checked her face. He must have noticed how harried she was that morning; she needed to watch it.

They were heading to the Rices' for dinner. Bea had demurred when Barb had called to invite her just before she left the Gardens–after all, they'd fed her brunch the day before–but Barb said they were "just grilling burgers. Veggie burgers, too," and Bea accepted gratefully. The kids leapt for the pool in borrowed swimsuits, and she was enjoying a Dos Equis, feeling relaxed for the first time since her early morning parking lot meditation.

John Rice was in commercial real estate and knew something about Alan and Myron Shandley's business. "I always understood that Liz and Myron co-owned the business, although she left all the work to him. So, he'll finally be able to do what he wants with it. I'm quite sure he'll want to get out of it as fast as possible. I wouldn't be surprised if he took the money and ran to New York or Paris or some other urban artsy spot. The Shandleys still have some good properties, because Alan got in during Tucson's post-war boom days. Frankly, this could be a fine opportunity for *our* shop."

"John, we are talking about a murder investigation, not a business opportunity," Barb protested.

"I did tell you that this was a murder investigation *in strictest confidence*," Bea said.

John looked at her in amusement. "You do realize that all your board and staff members are probably telling their spouses and best friends about the day's events right now—*in strictest confidence*, of course."

Bea didn't much like that thought.

"Who do *you* think did it?" Barb asked.

"God, I don't know. I truly hope it's somebody from the outside."

"Well. For what it's worth, Bea, I can't stand Buffy Jones. I see her at alumni events for Evans College. She's an insufferable snob, in my opinion."

"True enough," said Bea. "But Buffy and Liz were old, old friends from prep school days. They rode horses together in the desert all the time, despite being seventy-five or something. Or however old they really are, or were; that's just my guess, based on their hands, which haven't been surgically processed."

"I think Alan's obit said he was in his late seventies. That was what, five years ago?" asked John.

"Yes," Bea said, "I have to say that Buffy finally showed her age yesterday; she looked devastated. She blew her nose and dabbed her eyes all day. She was genuinely upset. And what good would it be to her to knock off her best buddy? I mean just because you don't like Buffy doesn't mean she's a psychopath, Barb."

"Okay, so let's talk about something pleasant. How's that writer you met at the potluck?"

"Barb, I am not ready for any real involvement right now. He's a nice guy, but frankly, the idea of serious dating—the idea of sex, Barb—makes me want to vomit. Literally."

"I'm guessing that's a temporary illness. So, have you seen him since you met him?"

Bea sighed. "We had a nice dinner at that new Mediterranean place. He asked about the divorce, and I told him the whole sorry tale. He had his own painful story. It happened a few years ago, but *he* never got married. And no kids. He claims he really likes being around them and that he dotes on his nephew and niece. He'll probably meet my kids on the next date. I guess we'll have a next date. He seems to get it that I need to go slowly."

"You haven't talked to him about the Shandley mess?"

"Nope."

"By morning, it'll be everywhere. Good luck."

* * *

That night Bea tried to will herself to sleep with positive thoughts. The only one that surfaced was that Marcia was the lead investigator, and she was a very competent woman. Their bond was more than childhood play; there had been an incident in junior high that caused them to have each other's backs in high school when their paths diverged. Bea had campaigned for Marcia as Student Body President even though her friends thought Marcia was too "straight." Once she got elected, Marcia had pressed the administration on Bea's friends' campaign to institute composting and recycling. But unspoken between Bea and Marcia was the story of the seventh-grade biology field trip.

Mr. Simmons was a handsome guy, the kind that inspires seventh-grade crushes. He was slim and blonde with surprising big brown eyes and high cheekbones. He took the kids on a biology camp out high up in the ponderosa pines of the Pinaleño Mountains a couple of hours from town. He and his wife were the only adults on the trip. The kids had never seen her before; Bea remembered her friends saying that it was too bad he was married. In retrospect, it seemed odd to Bea that there weren't more adults on the trip; but it had been a private school, without a lot of the rules she had dealt with as a public school teacher. Rules and regulations were *not* all bad.

The first night, Mr. Simmons "checked in" on the girls. There were only six girls in the class, so they fit into a giant tent. Mrs. Simmons was sleeping with them, but she wasn't there when he came by, without any warning. When Mr. Simmons put his head through the door, the girls were already in their pajamas, except for a very shy girl named Brenda. She'd just pulled off her shirt and her bra. When she shrieked, Mr. Simmons said, "It's just biology," and laughed, but he didn't apologize. As soon as he left, Marcia and Bea made another one of their pacts. They were not going to change into pajamas the next night at all. They'd sleep fully clothed, and they urged the rest of the girls to do the same. Nobody else had agreed on their plan—in fact, it seemed like a couple of the girls found the whole thing kind of titillating.

"Like he said, it's just *biology*," said one of the better-endowed twelve-year-olds.

Marcia snorted in disgust and Bea was marshalling arguments when Mrs. Simmons walked into the tent. The conversation stopped. The girls were far too young to discuss the whole thing with *her*.

Sure enough, the next night, Mr. Simmons headed over to "check in" at bedtime, while his wife was out. Marcia and Bea stood guard at the door, fully clothed, and told him everybody wasn't ready for bed yet. He looked annoyed, and he certainly didn't apologize for coming at a bad time either that night or the night before. By the time all the girls were in their sleeping bags Mrs. Simmons was back, and her husband came by again. She met him at the door, and they walked off together for a while.

When everybody got back to school, Marcia insisted that Bea had to come with her to tell the principal what happened. Bea remembered almost throwing up when they knocked on the principal's office door, but they did it together. Mr. Simmons ended up getting fired, and that was a good thing. It turned out a couple of girls on camp outs in earlier years had had a little more than "check-ins" with him. One of them had made a suicide attempt. The principal hadn't known the reason for the girl's attempt, and she hadn't even told her parents. The whole thing came out in the papers, the school instituted trainings for students and teachers, and Bea and Marcia were minor heroes.

Bea's parents were horrified by the whole story, and they'd taken her out of the private school and put her into the public junior high, thank God. Marcia's parents were the sort who downplayed the "incident" and would have doubted their daughter's word if the principal hadn't backed her up. In different schools, Bea and Marcia grew apart in the critical pre-high school years. But Bea knew the experience had shaped Marcia's life long after it was over.

"I want to go into law enforcement. I want to help people like Iris," Marcia had confided to her before she and Bea lost touch with each other. Iris was the girl who'd nearly killed herself and was now doing much better since her secret had come out.

The two old friends ended up in the same public high school by sophomore year. Even though they were in different cliques by then, there was that unspoken bond between them. Each knew the other had what it took to tell Mr. Simmons to wait to come in, and to knock on the principal's door.

Bea looked back on her twelve-year-old self with pride. She needed to get some of that confidence back. Some of that take-charge spirit. Somehow, she'd let Pat be the star in their marriage; some old tape from her mother about the primary breadwinner being the decision-maker. She'd taken a couple of years off from work after both births. When she'd returned to teaching, her salary was still low, while Pat's income had shot up. And Pat had that businessman's respect for those who earn good money and disrespect for those who make other choices. "You're taking an even *lower* salary?" he'd asked when she took the Shandley job.

Maybe the silver lining about this horrible investigation was that it would bring out the old Bea again, the intrepid person who was Marcia's partner in seeking justice.

CHAPTER SEVEN

Tuesday morning started in the deep dark. It was June 24th and they needed to be at the San Juan's Day celebration behind Native Delights to watch the sun rise at 5:20. Alicia was going to put on the celebration whether or not Shandley Gardens was in turmoil. About thirty people showed up at the kitchen gardens along the Tanque Verde Wash, rubbing the sleep out of their eyes and clutching various models of coffee mugs. Bea's had orange poppies and purple lupines on it; Andy and Jessie had hot chocolate in matching elephant mugs. Everyone was far too sleepy to ask gossipy questions about what was happening at the Gardens, thank God. Alicia was stirring a huge pot of white tepary beans on a camp stove. She looked as "take charge" this morning in jeans and sneakers, with a bandanna around her hair, as she did in her tailored pants suits and silk scarves. She was giving a little lecture to a rumpled assembly around the pot: "Yes, teparies grow wild around here, and they were domesticated by native people. Just like chiltipines."

Jessie picked up one of the blue tin cups next to the bean pot and handed it to Alicia, who shook her head. "Not yet." She gestured towards an old woman, an elder from the Pascua Yaqui Tribe, who said that it was time to bless the garden. The thirty onlookers had become forty; they gathered around the elder. Bea and the kids stood with Angus, who put Jessie on his shoulders so she could see better. Angus's wife Jean was there, too. She was talking to Jessie, and Bea had a sudden image of them with kids of their own. They would have been great parents. Angus had told her that they'd decided to live the lifestyle they wanted, which meant that a gardener and a singer/songwriter couldn't afford kids. Bea wondered if they'd ever regretted the decision. But Angus was a great uncle for her own children.

The small, wrinkled elder sprinkled water from a gourd, asking for rain. Then she blessed the four directions with an eagle feather. Everyone was silent. As the sun broke over the horizon, a line of Native American dancers filed out, and the motley audience—Native Americans of all ages, Anglo retirees, Anglo hippie families, Mexican-American college students, and assorted business people who were friends of Alicia's—watched respectfully as the sun began to shine on the dancers' bare limbs. Angus had put Jessie down, and she was stomping in time with their rattles, ready to join them if her mother let go of her hand. The dancers finished with a long chant.

Then breakfast was served. Tepary beans, mesquite/corn muffins with prickly pear jam, and watermelon. And more coffee. People were awake now and remarking on the morning coolness. "I should always take a walk at this time of the day in the summer," said one of the college students. Jessie brought a slice of watermelon to the elder, who gave her a hug. The June sun, which felt like a besieging army at midday, was peacefully warming in the early morning.

Bea hadn't needed to worry about spending this family time with the same cast of characters she'd been cloistered with during the previous day's interviews. Her fellow staff members were there—Ethan and Javier as well as Angus and Jean—but none of the board members made Alicia's celebration. Not even Dr. Ramos, who'd said it was a "fantastic idea." *That's just like him,* she thought, and then caught herself. Every uncharitable wish now made her halfway suspect certain people of murder. She needed this part of her life to change quickly. The board members probably weren't here because they never got up early. They never had to.

It seemed time to go, and she started to herd the kids into the car when Andy stopped her. "We can't leave now, Mom! We'll miss the water fight!"

"I told him not to miss this part, Bea," said Angus.

Out came the balloons; this was another way of bringing on the rains. Somebody who worked for Alicia had been
hiding a stash of filled water balloons, their necks twisted
shut and tied with paperclips. Angus grabbed one, removed
the paper clip, and sent it straight towards Andy, soaking
several people in its wake. Andy reciprocated quickly; Bea
hadn't even seen him get a balloon. Jessie dumped a cup of
water down Angus's shirt. He had pretended not to notice
her approach, but he grabbed her by the legs, threw her over
his shoulder, and ran off with her, a shrieking, delighted bun-
dle. So far, Bea had managed to stand off to the side, staying dry. Javier had joined in the action; he seemed to have a
couple of old friends at the event, and all were lobbing balloons with expert aim. Ethan made a half-hearted entry into
the group, throwing a cup of water at Bea's now saturated
son, but Ethan wasn't too good at play. She knew he had no
children, and maybe no siblings. At least he was joining in.
Suddenly Alicia came up behind Bea and dumped a cup of
water on her feet. Bea got her back, and in a moment they
both had wet hair.

Andy and Jessie got into the car soaked from head to toe,
but Bea knew that all of them would be dry—hair included—
by the time they got across town, especially with the windows down and the air conditioning off. Tucson summers
were, after all, only a "dry heat," a term meant to discount
the red-hot temperatures. Yes, it was dry, and it was already
getting uncomfortably hot.

"Mom, we do a lot more fun stuff since you got this job,"
Andy asserted in the car.

Bea thought maybe she *had* made a good choice in working at Shandley after all. The kids were gaining an extended
family that was a lot more fun than most biological ones.
She got her children to camp dry and on time, both of which
seemed miraculous.

As she pulled into the Shandley parking lot ready to deal
with whatever came her way, she took some deep breaths
and started to settle into her meditation. Her calm dissipated, though, when she saw that the police cruisers were

already there. Again. She sighed and tried to think of a positive. Well, at least Shandley would be closed to the public, given Ethan's press release. She got out of the car without meditating a bit.

They probably needed a "Closed today; sorry for the inconvenience" sign in the parking lot and on the front door. People *would* show up. The volunteers who worked on the grounds would still be coming in, even if the ones who took admissions and the ones who gave tours would have the day off. *Thank God for the volunteers*, she thought, as a Burger King wrapper blew from the parking lot into the cactus garden and got stuck on an organ pipe cactus. They'd keep the place cleaned up and the plants watered in this horrendous weather. It was supposed to hit 110 degrees again today.

There was a note on her office door to go see Marcia, who was back in the cop room with Officer Blake. Marcia had more breaking news, unfortunately.

"Bea, I don't know if you know that there was a rope involved in this crime. We found rope burns on the fatal branch. Somebody got up in the tree and tied it and then pulled the branch down on Liz Shandley," Marcia said.

Bea nodded cautiously.

"Did your friend Angus tell you this, too?"

Another nod.

"We typically let facilities with big dumpsters in the area know when we're looking for stuff. The rope was in the dumpster of your local Circle K. No fingerprints. But it matches the one missing from Shandley's tool shed. Javier and Angus have both confirmed that. Unfortunately, we can't find any footprints in the leaf litter under the eukes either. But it's really odd. It's like somebody is trying to leave us clues—first the mosaic with the rose through her teeth and the rose pin on her blouse, then this. It was under the eukes." She held up a little enamel brooch covered with red tulips. "Okay, Bea, what's with the tulips and the roses?"

"Oh."

"What do you mean, 'oh'?"

"Well, you heard about the lawn, right?"

"From your boss. Part of the board retreat was to look at putting the new Events Center on the lawn area. And reduce the lawn. People were in agreement, it was all sweetness and light, everything was coming up roses."

That was the Marcia she remembered.

"Well, see... the thing is that we use too much water here, and some of us—the staff, and Dr. Ramos, and Alicia—wanted to cut down on our water use by getting rid of the lawn."

"Yes, Myron let me know that he thought Armando Ramos leaked the garden's water use figures to *The Tucson Post* to pressure them into changing. It seems unlikely to me, because those figures are a matter of public record, but I must say Dr. Ramos is not a popular guy. He made quite sure that I knew the principles of xeriscaping, which he went on at some length to explain, is not *zero*scaping."

Bea laughed at this. Marcia was a native Tucsonan. She was not a tourist who didn't know what xeriscaping was. She knew *xeri* meant dry.

"Anyway," Marcia continued, "Dr. Ramos wanted to make sure that I understood that no self-respecting gardener following the principles of xeriscaping could have more than 10% in high-water-use plants. And that it was sometimes hard for him to be on a board with people who can be 'so clueless about basic issues like this.' But line it out for me... what does this have to do with tulips?"

"Marcia, it's not just the *lawn* that's high-water use. There's the rose garden and the tulip bed, too. Plus, the tropical greenhouse. Buffy and Myron won't budge on changing any of these areas, and Liz was the firmest of all on this stuff. Alan was a fantastic rose gardener, and he loved tulips. There are some rare varieties. Angus and Dr. Ramos, especially, want to cut that area down a lot and put in some other desert plants. Alicia likes the idea of changing it into an ethnobotany garden—you know, one with plants for food and shelter and medicine, that sort of thing."

"Kind of like a kitchen garden for her restaurants?" Officer Blake contributed this.

"If you mean that in a pleasant, non-literal way."

Marcia raised her eyebrows again. "Back to roses and tulips."

"Well, there's nothing to say, really. Except that it's not worth killing somebody because a person wants to tear out her dead husband's rose and tulip garden. I mean, a lot of us care about saving more water, but not *that* much, Marcia."

"Well, somebody is obsessed with roses and tulips, I'd say. And they want us to know it." Marcia curled her lip at that last statement. Meanwhile, Officer Blake put on some gloves and pulled the Liz mosaic out of the supply closet. They must have moved it from Angus's office. Bea wished she didn't have to see it again. Her first instinct was to look away.

"Look at this, Bea. Does anything stand out to you now, a couple of days after the first shock is over?"

"It's Liz because of the cleft in her chin. She looks younger. And it's kind of cartoonish."

"Yes, it wasn't done by anyone who wished her well. If it was done by the tree puller, that's obvious. But maybe the artist and the murderer are two separate people."

"In cahoots?"

"Could be," Marcia said.

"Do you know any mosaic artists in the Garden community?" Officer Blake said this in his usual harsh way.

"No. Well... no."

They waited. Blake's hands were poised over the laptop keyboard.

"I know Javier's wife Maria does some nice mosaics on clay pots and mirrors and things like that. They're pretty, not satirical."

"Tell us about Maria," Blake said.

"She's in Mexico right now!"

"Tell us about Maria." This time Marcia asked.

"She was the Shandleys' housekeeper. She still cleans this building on a contract basis. But she's at a funeral in Mexico for a week. She's been gone for days! She wasn't in town when Liz fell!"

"You think Maria's a good person and couldn't be involved," Blake said. His tone was neutral, but his pursed lips showed disdain.

"Maria is a quiet, hard-working woman. Marcia, she's like the mother of lots of kids we went to school with. She doesn't want to make trouble with the Anglo community, not because she's undocumented, but because she doesn't want to stand out. She probably knows people who *could* get deported, and she doesn't want to endanger anybody. She minds her own business, makes some yard art on the side, enjoys her grandchildren. But hey... Myron's an artist. I suppose he might make mosaics, but I have no idea."

"Now you're finally not standing up for somebody," Marcia said, but it was gentle teasing. Not disdain. "Okay, there are just two people left I need to ask you about. First, Buffy Jones."

"Well, she and her husband came to Tucson about the same time as Liz and her husband. And I hear that both couples got rich from Tucson's post-World War II growth."

"The Shandleys were in real estate, correct?" Officer Blake had been taking notes steadily.

"Yes, and the Joneses were in hotels and resorts," Bea said.

"And Gregory Jones died a couple of years ago, of brain cancer," Blake said.

"Well, I wouldn't know about that. But I can tell you that once Buffy did tell me something personal. She saw me with my friend Barb Rice, and she said that she was pleased that she and Liz had rediscovered their girlhood friendship in their widowhood. She said they were both close to Myron, too."

"Do you have anything else to tell us about her, Bea?" Why did Officer Blake always make her feel guilty?

"Okay. Buffy seems excited about contributing the Jones Event Center to Shandley Gardens. Sometimes she seems to care more about the Gardens than either Liz or Myron."

"And Alicia Vargas?" This was Marcia. Officer Blake was busy typing something.

"Alicia's a competent board president. Part of Tucson's Country Club set, like the other two, but she's younger. She hasn't had so many nips and tucks, though, so she looks closer to her age."

"I believe there was a lawsuit between the Vargases and the Shandleys," Blake said.

"Well, yeah, I guess Alan nearly put the Vargases out of business when he evicted them from a couple of his properties, supposedly for a higher paying tenant," Bea said. "An Anglo tenant, I'm pretty sure. He might have been able to get away with that then. It was a long time ago, maybe in the seventies. The Vargases sued, and I think they settled out of court. A volunteer told me all this. I'm sure you can find it out without asking me."

"Yes, we're just interested in your take on it," Officer Blake said.

"Thanks, Bea, you've been a great help. I knew you would be," Marcia said.

"Marcia, I have a question for you."

"Shoot."

"Why did Liz go walking under that tree when there was a break in the retreat? She knew eucalyptus are dangerous in the wind. What a weird thing to do."

"Good, Bea. You're thinking the right way. Her cell phone shows the record of a call from a burner phone earlier on Sunday, before anybody was at Shandley. We don't know who it was, but we think they may have told her to walk down that way for a treat, or a surprise, or something, after the first part of the meeting."

"And she did it because she knew them."

"That would make sense. It could have been someone close to her, or maybe not."

"And she did think she was due special treats. Sorry, that was uncalled-for," she added as Officer Blake looked up at her from his notes. "Well, I can see how that mosaic would have beckoned her to walk where she did, but seeing it was no treat. Nor was what happened next. And I'm sure it would have distracted her from noticing that there was someone up in the tree. Or did they pull down the branch from the bottom? I still can't believe any of this is happening."

"But it is. We think they pulled the branch down from below, on the ground, after it had been partially sawed through."

"Yuck."

"Okay, Bea, you can go. Thanks again," said Marcia.

Bea walked out with the sinking feeling that she had cast doubt upon several people. Angus, Maria, Dr. Ramos. Maybe Ethan? And Alicia. She needed to get ahead of Marcia's questioning. She needed to figure this out. She couldn't imagine any of them committing murder, but she was more loyal to some of the "suspects" than others. Angus and Javier were both her friends and her colleagues, and she thought they were above board. Damn it.

CHAPTER EIGHT

Bea's new friend Frank *had* checked in with the rest of the world long enough to realize that Shandley Gardens was in the news. He called right when Bea got home to offer his condolences for Liz's death—he thought maybe they were close. Clearly, he didn't know Bea too well yet.

"That's not the only tragedy, Frank. Okay, you have to promise to keep this to yourself."

"Sure, Bea, what?"

"There's a murder investigation going on at the Gardens. Thankfully, Ethan has closed the place for the next couple of days. I really hope the whole thing is wrapped up by then. Except I don't really. Because the cops think it was one of us—a board or staff member. At least I'm off the hook."

Frank exhaled quickly. "Bea, how about if I pick up a roasted chicken and a bottle of wine? Andy and Jessie like chicken, right?"

"Yes. Okay. I'll make a salad and I have some good bread. And ice cream. We need ice cream."

They had a reasonably comfortable meal together. Bea was nervous about the kids' reaction to him, but of course, Jessie jumped into Frank's lap right away. Andy kept his distance, and asked Frank how long he was staying. "'Cause sometimes my daddy's girlfriends stay all night."

At this, Frank gave Bea a questioning look. She caught it out of the corner of her eye, because she was looking down. She didn't want Andy to see how shocked she was. She wasn't shocked that Pat had a girlfriend, but his daddy's girl*friends*? Plural? Around the kids? What was going on at Pat's house, anyway? She needed to talk to him. *After* they got this murder solved, when she could focus on talking with Pat calmly.

She was trying to find the right words to say to Andy, when Frank jumped in and assured him that he'd "leave after your mom and I have a little time to talk after you guys go to bed." This was a relief. Bea had no desire to navigate the stress of dating on top of the tension at work. And she didn't need Andy to have a meltdown just now either.

The wine was a nice cold chardonnay, un-oaked. Frank remembered from their dinner at the Mediterranean place that she hated the oaky kind. And he listened well while she talked. It didn't seem faked. He asked some good questions.

"It sounds like you're telling me that everybody there disliked Liz. Is that right?"

"No. I think Myron and Buffy really cared for her. Although Liz smothered Myron. I don't know how he could stand it. But he was always solicitous of his mother, and they hung out together a lot. With Buffy, too."

"And what about your boss? Did he secretly despise the board president?"

"Oh, I'm never sure what he thinks of anyone. He could hate us all, for all I know, but he's unfailingly polite to everyone. I do know he loves plants."

"So that leaves a lot of people who don't like her. Javier, right? And Maria, but you say she's in Mexico, and the cops can verify that. She could have made the mosaic before she went to Mexico, though, even if she wasn't around when Liz was killed. And Angus. And Alicia. I doubt she's *really* forgiven her for that lawsuit, don't you?"

"It seems unlikely that she actually *liked* Liz on that basis, I agree. But she is a consummate professional. And she does like gardens, so it kind of makes sense that she's on the board."

"Then here's Dr. Ramos. What's his first name, anyway? You call everybody else by their first name."

"Armando."

"And then there's you."

"Well, Marcia said I'm off the hook. I hope that stands!"

"Yeah, let's hope you stay that way. And who knows,

maybe the people who act like they loved Liz feel entirely differently."

"Well, I sure hope more people get off the suspect list soon. This is unbearable."

"Pretty damned interesting, though!"

She could see the writer's mind kicking into gear. "Frank, this is not a novel you're writing! This is my life, and it's stressful!"

"Sorry, Bea. I get that."

His hand slid her hair back from her face, gently, and he looked her in the eye. "Goodnight."

Good, no kiss goodnight. Easier that way.

"I told Andy I wouldn't stay long." And then he was gone.

Bea hadn't meant for him to make *that* quick an exit. But maybe it was a good thing he had. Andy was standing in his bedroom door, pulling on his ear. "Mama, I can't sleep."

And so she put him to bed, and stroked his forehead until he fell asleep.

As she pulled on her nightshirt, she found herself wondering why she was so nervous about getting involved with Frank. He seemed like a genuinely nice human being. And he came well recommended; one of her closest Santa Cruz friends had gone to med school with him at the University of Virginia. They were both older students, so that bond had made them friends and study partners. When Frank moved to Tucson, his study partner told him to give Bea a call. She'd written Bea a long email about the guy. Frank had been an English major at a small liberal arts school in New England. He'd spent quite a few years after graduating traveling the world and then the U.S., taking seasonal jobs with the Forest Service and the Park Service. Bea's friend said he was plenty competent for medical school, but his heart wasn't in it. He was just doing what was expected of him; he came from a long line of prominent Virginia physicians. His heart *was* in writing, and in hiking and camping in the wilderness, and he'd decided to try making Tucson the center of both endeavors.

"He's perfect for you," Barb Rice had said, and Bea had to

admit that Frank sounded refreshing. The image she had of her romantic life was a house burned down by a forest fire, surrounded by blackened trees. But she knew there were green woods out there somewhere, beyond the wreckage.

Except it sounded like Frank was a little footloose. He had nothing really tying him to Tucson right now, and who knew what personal connections he had with other places. He could be a freelancer anywhere. And who knew how he felt about kids in his life? Yeah, he'd been good with Andy, but people who'd never been parents were almost always shocked by the 24/7 nature of the task. He liked freedom, that was clear from his life choices. Well, it was early days in the relationship. He might not be worth taking any major risks. She had to be careful, and she would be.

Bea knew her reticence had more to do with her ex-husband than with Frank. She'd figured that having two kids with Pat ensured that they were committed, for life, and yet he'd lost interest in her when she became dependent on his help and his income in a way she'd never been when she'd been devoted to her career. Maybe this was what "catch and release" fish felt like. Probably not, they were probably simply delighted to be thrown back into the currents. She was, too—she really was. She was better off this way. She was sure of one thing: she wasn't going to let them all be reeled in and thrown out again.

Bea awoke a little earlier than usual the next morning and thought she'd steal a cup of coffee and look at the paper before waking the kids. She knew the police were done at the Gardens and had gone back to the station, and she'd be able to conduct her parking lot meditation in peace. Since Shandley Gardens was closed to the public, she wouldn't have to oversee volunteer tours and the children's summer program she was supposed to have taught. Her calm lasted until she glanced at the front page of the paper.

There it was. "Murder at Shandley Gardens." The only reason the story wasn't above the fold was that a certain politician, not a favorite of the newspaper's editorial page, had just been indicted for corruption. Still, a murder on the front page below the fold was bad enough for Shandley. The story featured a picture of Liz at some gala, jewels anywhere they could be affixed, smiling prettily for the camera.

Bea wondered briefly who had tipped the reporter off to the murder investigation. She knew it could have been any one of the friends, relatives or acquaintances of the board and staff, people who'd been sworn to secrecy. She hoped it wasn't the Rices. Probably not. At any rate, headaches awaited the staff at Shandley. And she was also going to have to tell Andy and Jessie about this. Who knew what the kids at camp would say?

The *Post* speculated that Liz and Alan had made several enemies as they rose to prominence in Tucson, mentioning the lawsuit with Alicia and Raoul Vargas years ago, when they'd been forced out of their first restaurant building. Raoul had called Alan a "g.d. bigot." This made it even more surprising that Alicia and Liz had seemed to get along so well on the Shandley board. Things could get horrible fast now that the news of the murder was out. Bea didn't think it could possibly be good to have Shandley's dirty laundry plastered all over the internet, no matter what people said about the benefits of "increasing your profile."

It was time to get her children up.

Before they'd finished their last spoonfuls of granola, Bea finally broached the issue.

"You guys, people have found out that Mrs. Shandley didn't die by accident. It's awful, but it seems like somebody made that branch fall down on her on purpose."

Andy's eyes widened. "Mom, are you talking about *murder?*"

"Right now it looks that way."

Andy started pulling on his ear in earnest. Jessie looked at him and then at her mother with a fearful expression that made Bea furious that she had to expose them to all this.

"Don't worry, you two. Nobody's after me. If anybody bugs you about it, please let your teacher or the camp director know." Jessie ran into her arms, and Bea collected Andy into the hug.

She tried to put on a good show of calm and good cheer as she packed their lunches and got them to the camp bus. She pulled into the Shandley parking lot with dread, which increased when she saw the Channel 2 News truck they used for live broadcasts. A big-haired reporter in a very short dress was trying to shove a microphone in Marcia's face. A cameraman was moving in on her, as well. Marcia backed up a couple of steps and said she was unable to comment on an ongoing investigation. Ethan was standing next to Marcia. When the microphone and camera homed in on him, he was calm and official. "Liz Shandley's death is a terrible tragedy. The police are doing their best to discover what happened. I have no information for you. We at Shandley will do everything we can to help the police with their investigation."

The reporter pressed her lips together into a thin line, but then she turned her head towards Bea, who was heading for the front door. She feared the reporter would figure out she must have some official capacity at Shandley, since the place wasn't yet open to the public. Bea looked over her shoulder. As the reporter was advancing on her, she broke into an almost-run, got to her office in record time, and locked the door. The reporter had apparently stayed outside, trying to get more out of Ethan and Marcia.

She stared out her window at a couple of clouds low on the horizon. Maybe they would turn into something good and wash down this whole sordid mess. The third front-page story that morning said that Tucson had already broken some June temperature records.

There was, of course, a downside to not having volunteers at the Gardens that day. She'd had to cancel the meeting about the patio garden tour, which was only a week away. Ethan wanted it done well. When she turned on her computer, she found that a key tour volunteer was quitting until the murder was solved, because she "didn't feel safe" being involved with Shandley until then. Two of the prime patio garden owners asked if the tour couldn't be put off. It probably could, despite the advance publicity and all the arrangements. But an email from her boss dispelled that notion. "WE WILL NOT PUT OFF THE TOUR," it announced on the subject line. He said that they couldn't afford to break their contracts with the caterers and the transportation company. "We need the money, Bea. Do what you can to calm everybody down," he wrote.

But would the public show up for this fundraiser with the Gardens under such a cloud?

Scrolling further through her emails provided an answer for that question. They were now overbooked. Curiosity had probably trumped any fears the customers had. Now Bea just had to make sure they had an event to come to.

Angus stopped by her office. "How's the party planning business going?"

"Oh, I don't know. It'll happen."

"I have visions of us turning into a sort of wedding Disneyland. Not what I got a horticulture degree for. There are other gardens who don't prostitute themselves this way."

"Yes, and they have big endowments. Liz didn't leave us one. Unless there's one in her will."

"Don't count on that. I have to say, I don't agree with Armando Ramos about much, but I agree with him that Liz should have endowed this place when she turned it public. He seems to hold out hope that this elusive endowment is in her will. I think Ethan has the same hope, but he's quieter about it."

"I think *you* should keep quiet about anything you didn't like about Liz, Angus."

He rolled his eyes and left.

Bea sighed. Did Marcia need to know that some people were angry with Liz about not providing an endowment? She could mention it. For all she knew, the whole board felt that way. Although she doubted anybody but the real plant guys, like Ramos and Angus, thought that making money from parties was "prostituting" the place.

But there was no hope of concentrating on work. Someone was shrieking outside Ethan's office. A woman was yelling, "Look at this, Ethan! In my own courtyard!" Bea opened her door a crack. It was Buffy. With another mosaic, it looked like. Bea opened the door a little wider. Ethan was saying, "It's all right, Buffy, just put it down, we'll call the police." She dropped the thing on the floor, and Ethan pulled her inside his office gently and closed the door. Bea didn't move until she was sure that Buffy wasn't going to rush back out. She could hear Ethan's reassuring tone, if not his words, and Buffy's gasping breaths were becoming quieter.

Bea walked over to look at the mosaic. Buffy had left it face up, so Bea didn't have to touch the thing. It was a young Liz again, her face framed by white trumpet-shaped flowers. The kind favored by Georgia O'Keeffe, but this was no O'Keeffe masterpiece. The flowers looked like they were supposed to be datura, a common plant around Tucson. And a highly toxic one. It had to be the same "artist" who'd made the first mosaic: same one-color Mexican mosaic tile pieces, same plywood backing.

After a few minutes, her phone rang. It was Ethan. He probably didn't want to leave Buffy for a minute. "Bea, I'm sure you heard Buffy. Would you mind bringing her a cup of tea while we wait for the police?" Marcia must have gone back to the station after that press conference.

"I'd be glad to, Ethan." Bea would like to do something useful since she clearly wasn't going to get much done on the fundraiser. She went out to the staff kitchenette and made some Earl Grey in a flowered mug. *Buffy must have been really traumatized to bring the mosaic to Ethan instead of calling the cops herself,* she thought.

By the time the tea was ready, there was no mosaic in the hallway.

Bea knocked on the cop room door. A faint voice barely recognizable as Buffy's told her to come in.

"Thank you, Bea, dear," she said. Her hands shook as she took the mug. She gestured over to the datura mosaic, which was leaning against the wall. "Who do you suppose created this monstrous thing?"

"I wish I could tell you that."

"Yes," was all Buffy said, and she looked down at her tea. Bea knew she was being dismissed.

Bea kept her office door open, and she saw Marcia in the hallway. She stuck her head in Bea's door and said, "Don't go anywhere. I want to talk to you about this."

What did that mean?

Marcia knocked on the cop room door and entered. After twenty minutes or so, Buffy emerged. Bea still had her door ajar. "Thanks for the tea, Bea," she said. She had a little more color in her cheeks, but she still looked terrible. Ethan's door must have been open, too, because Buffy said, "Ethan, I appreciate the moral support."

He responded, "Of course," but she was already headed for the front door off the boardroom. Bea wondered if Buffy was in any shape to drive and if she should follow her, when Marcia pushed into her office without knocking. She looked decidedly annoyed.

"Okay, come talk to me about datura."

Bea followed her without a word. Marcia shut the cop room door with a bang.

"I think you plant people need to get a life. Roses between the teeth, rose pins, tulip pins, now huge daturas. What's the deal? I know datura's poisonous. Everybody around here knows that. We pick up teenagers who experiment with it every year. Usually they come out all right, but a couple of times it's been fatal. Not only that, Bea; a kid just last week lost his vision for three days after eating the stuff in a salad. So damn it, Bea, what's the deal with datura in this picture?"

"Well, *this* isn't a high-water-use plant. Maybe it's not about the fight over getting rid of the roses and tulips." *That would be good. It'd get Angus off the hook.*

Marcia just looked at her. "So... tell me about datura."

"Well, obviously, you know it's a common native plant and it's very toxic. Different plants have different levels of toxicity, so that makes it especially dangerous to experiment with. It's also called Devils' Trumpet and Jimsonweed, which apparently is short for 'Jamestown weed.' The Jamestown settlers got high on it. Also, I guess witches used it. And Indian mystics."

"Great. So, what does it have to do with Liz?"

"Maybe somebody thought she was witchy?"

"Somebody is leading us around by the nose, and I do not like it at all. Whoever it is has done an excellent job of keeping their fingerprints off of everything, too. This thing seems to be made of broken Mexican tiles, like the last one. You said that Maria makes things with tiles?"

"Yes, but she's in Mexico."

"We know that. We've confirmed it. But we're going to get a warrant to search Javier's house."

"Oh, no!"

"He's not accused of anything at the moment. But we did find out something interesting when we did some digging about the Shandley property. Did you know that Javier's family owned the original *rancho* here? They were homesteaders in the mid-nineteenth century."

"No, he never mentioned it."

"Well, you might ask him about it. Like a lot of small farmers, they couldn't make it when the big Anglo land and cattle companies bought up huge tracts of land. They had to sell out and move to town."

"You don't mean Alan Shandley bought out Javier's family!"

"No, no. There was a huge ranch here in between, from about nineteen-twenty until the place was broken up and sold. Alan bought his forty acres in the fifties. This parcel was where the big landowners had a dude ranch, bringing in Easterners wanting a comfortable Wild West experience."

"We should have some signage about all this here. People would be interested in the history."

"Let's concentrate on this murder, Bea. I just wondered if you'd heard anything about this background story—it's something board members might want to cover up. Lots of Mexican ranchers weren't rousted out by simple economics; violence and trickery were sometimes involved."

"It looks like you're trying to get me to find more of a motive for Javier to have killed Liz."

"We're all just gathering information right now, Bea. Thanks for your help with that. I need to get back to the station with this lovely mosaic."

This time, Marcia's thanks didn't make her feel any better.

She managed to calm down one of the two patio garden homeowners who'd wanted out. She'd work on the other one, a fidgety older woman, the next day. Except she couldn't. She had to go to Phoenix for a botanical garden meeting. Damn.

Bea had a very bad rest of her day. The day camp had a lice epidemic, and some were found in Jessie's hair. Bea was instructed to buy lice shampoo, shampoo both kids with it, wash anything that had touched Jessie's head, and ABSOLUTELY NOT send the kids back unless she was sure they were clean. She spent the evening combing dead lice and nits out of Jessie's hair.

When the kids were finally in bed, Frank called, and she told him not to come over.

"Bea, did you read the obit in the morning paper?" he asked.

"No, but I heard about it. Liz was quite the charity queen, I guess. Ethan was surprised at all the groups she belonged to. He's probably worried that she's going to give to the symphony or the arts council instead of to us. In her will, I mean."

"Yeah. But she went to Davenport School!"

"What on earth difference does that make? That's her prep school, right? Some horsey place?" Frank was the last person Bea had expected to be impressed by prep-school lineage. They hadn't gotten to the high-school stories part of their courtship yet. If it was a courtship.

But it turned out he had a good reason for mentioning the prep school. "Bea, my mother went to Davenport!"

"Your point is?"

"She's about Liz's age, I think. Mom graduated from high school in the early fifties. She had me pretty late in life."

"Well, that's about right, probably. Ethan told me that the obit said Liz was eighty years old. And Angus told me that earlier. She sure didn't look it." Then Bea realized Frank's enthusiasm could get out of hand. "If you talk to your mother, just tell her that Liz died, okay? Not that somebody killed her."

"Bea, did you forget? I'm going back to Virginia for a few days. Leaving Friday. It's my mom's seventy-seventh birthday."

"Oh. Yes, I guess I forgot." Bea felt oddly crestfallen about this. She'd just proved to herself how little she knew him, after all. He'd told her a little more of his biography than she'd gotten from her friend the study partner: he was getting by on freelance journalism and grant writing while he was working on a novel. He was close to his mother; and his father, who'd been prominent in Virginia politics, had died young... at sixty. Frank had sounded sheepish when he said that he'd gone to medical school to honor his father, but that had been a "wrong turn." She loved the fact that even though the desert was new to Frank, he was enchanted by it. He wasn't even complaining about the June heat as much as some natives did. All that was a plus. But she had to admit that what she most appreciated was his comforting presence in the middle of all this craziness. She imagined him in her mind's eye. His curly black hair was already growing a bit gray around the ears. He wasn't tall, really just a few inches taller than she was. Okay, they were both short. But he was solid, and muscular. He was religious about going to the gym, she knew, and it showed. His long-lashed brown eyes looked at her with sympathy. He was reassuring, that's what Frank was.

And so she asked him for reassurance. "Frank, please don't tell your mom that this is about a murder."

"Sure. I'll say a good friend's board president died, and I thought Mom might know her."

"Okay." *A good friend, huh. Interesting. I wouldn't have gone that far in describing our relationship, but I like it. I do like it that he said that.*

"By the way, Bea, I think I ran into Myron Shandley today. I was at that all-you-can-eat diner on South Campbell. There was a guy at the next table with a receding hairline, sixtyish, tall, kind of pale and flabby."

"That could be Myron."

The restaurant owner came running up to apologize that

it had taken so long for this guy to get his bill. He came in when I did, and I hadn't gotten mine either, by the way. The owner kept saying, "I'm so sorry, Mr. Shandley, I'm happy to comp you." Mr. Shandley hesitated, but just then the waiter showed up with the bill, and the guy paid it, with a flourish. The owner was all over himself with thanks."

"Yeah, it sounds like Myron. In more ways than one."

"He does seem to think a lot is due him." He hesitated a moment. "Listen, Bea, I know you're tired, but I did find out something else."

"What now?"

"I found an article about the Vargases from a few years ago, when they won a Chamber of Commerce award. Alicia's family has been here for a long time, since the late eighteen-hundreds. They were one of the most successful middle-class business families of their day. Do you remember a furniture store called *Escalante's*?"

"Yeah, it didn't go out of business that long ago."

"Exactly. So, Alicia's family 'made it' in the greater community long ago. Raoul Vargas's family members were successful restaurateurs, but only in South Tucson. They didn't break into the circle of big time Tucson businesses. But Alicia and Raoul created restaurants that are putting Tucson on the national gastronomic map, as you know."

"Frank, as you mentioned, I'm exhausted. What is the point of this bit of history?"

"Well, the article mentioned that they had successfully sued to allow Hispanics into the Cactus Club. Even if Alicia's family's businesses were patronized by Tucson's elite, they didn't want to integrate the Cactus Club until she and Raoul pushed it."

"I still don't see why you're telling me all of this."

"Because I looked up that lawsuit, just for the hell of it. The primary Cactus Club antagonists to this lawsuit were Alan and Liz Shandley."

Bea's head was starting to hurt. "So, you think Alicia could have killed her as payback for that *now?*"

"Bea, I have no idea. It was interesting. Use it or not as

you see fit."

"I do not see fit. And I need to go to sleep, Frank. I need to get off the phone. I have to drive to Phoenix tomorrow."

"Sorry to hear that, Bea. Whatever for?"

"There's a meeting of botanical garden educators up there. I just hope we don't get big winds again."

"Take care of yourself, Bea."

She said she would, but she was a little curt in her good-bye. Maybe that wasn't fair; he seemed to be trying to help. But now she knew that the Vargases had sued the Shandleys *twice;* once over the eviction, and once over the Cactus Club policies.

Maybe it wasn't such a good deal that she and Marcia had been childhood friends. She didn't like a lot of the information she was accumulating.

CHAPTER NINE

It was already eighty-five and pre-monsoon muggy when Bea shoveled the kids into the car to go to the bus stop. They'd gotten up extra early so Bea could check their hair again for lice. Andy was clean, and after a few minutes of combing Bea sincerely hoped that her little girl was completely nit-free.

Anvil-shaped thunderheads were already forming on the horizon. This would be encouraging, except that there was only a twenty percent chance of rain. Usually they'd have to go through days of this, with the humidity rising every day before it poured. And even people *not* involved in a murder investigation were on edge at this time of year.

Couldn't this horrible investigation have happened in the winter, when Tucson's weather couldn't be beat, and people walked around smiling, smugly mentioning emails from relatives struggling with shoveling snow on dark northern afternoons? No, it would be worse in winter. There would be even more people interested in Shandley's crisis.

Bea didn't have to leave for Phoenix until mid-morning. She was able to do her parking lot meditation uninterrupted. She was just turning on her computer when Javier barged into her office without knocking, which was unusual. He was a strong, calm man, growing gray gracefully, with high cheekbones and an aquiline nose. But today he, like all of them, had lost his composure. It seemed he had good reason to.

"Bea, they think I killed Liz! I know you're friends with the lady cop. Please say something to her!"

"Hold on, Javier. Angus thinks they think *he* did it. Why you, now?"

"They searched my house. They had a warrant. I had to let them in. And they took away pieces of Maria's tiles in the workroom, and I heard them say there was a match with some of the ones on that thing we saw in the eukes. But that's easy, right? Maria just gets them from the Mexican tile store; they give her the broken ones. The patterns are really common. Anybody could get them. Anyway, the ones on the picture of Liz were one-color tiles. Talk about common!" He took a breath. "And there is some other picture, too? I didn't know about that. Something about datura. And they know Maria has been in Mexico, so she couldn't have brought those horrible pictures to Shandley. But I'm pretty sure they think I could have brought them! I guess one was at Mrs. Jones's house? And they think Maria still could have made them! Or I could have made them. You have to do something, Bea!"

"Javier, why on earth would anybody think you wanted to kill Liz?"

"I don't know why! Liz wasn't a friend, like Alan, but she kept me on here. I didn't hate her!" At this point, Javier seemed to realize he needed to sound calmer. He took a breath and looked Bea straight in the eye. "Bea, this place is more than a paycheck to me. You know I've put thirty years into it. It's my creation, mine and Alan's. Why would I want to kill Liz, the person who made sure I was hired here when we went public? Why would I want to wreck my life?"

"Javier, sit down and let's talk about what we can do."

"Bea, you better have some good ideas," he said in a new measured tone.

"Marcia mentioned that she knew your ancestors used to own this property."

"Well, yes, this was part of it. My great-grandfather sold it more than eighty years ago. What does that have to do with anything?"

"Probably nothing."

He was getting agitated again. "Of course it's nothing! I love to grow plants. So did my great-grandfather and lots of other people in my family and other people's families. I love the desert and I have a special feeling for the Rincon

Mountain foothills because I have history here. Don't tell me that all of that could convict me of murder!"

"Javier, calm down. They haven't arrested you yet. Somebody could have stolen those tiles from you... from Maria. Maybe to frame you. Or it could just be coincidence. You're right—the ones used in those mosaics are every-where."

"Bea." Javier took another deep breath. "Who could hate me so much they would want to frame me? Everybody always compliments me on my work. And they know I was close to Alan. I just can't understand who would do this to me. I just can't." He looked down at the floor. Bea figured he was embarrassed at being so emotional. But she was glad he trusted her.

"Well, I sure don't know who would want to frame you, Javier, but I'll think about it. Tell me if you have an idea about it, and I'll tell Marcia. And like I said, it's probably just coin-cidence."

Javier gave her a dubious look and left, pulling on his work gloves. Bea briefly considered cancelling her trip to Phoenix. But at this point, she could use the distraction.

Ethan stuck his head in her door. "Liz's memorial ser-vice will be held at the big Episcopal Church on Craycroft on Saturday at 11:00."

Saturday. This Is Wednesday.

"Also, Myron is the executor of the will. I'll be meeting with him about it tomorrow."

And you'll find out just how much Shandley Gardens meant to Liz.

* * *

It was now time for her to go to Phoenix to discuss the latest techniques in manufacturing interpretive signage. This seemed inconsequential at the moment. However it might be her only chance to forget the murder mess. So, she climbed into her Toyota and headed for the freeway. The "check engine" light went on again. She probably just had a loose gas cap, and it would go off eventually. Just one more thing. To worry about. She called her friend Sue, whom she was supposed to pick up, and asked her to drive. Sue couldn't. The check engine light went off. More living dangerously.

After a few stoplights she focused on the interior of her car. The seat was covered with school papers, empty and probably leaking juice boxes, and some dirty stones that Andy had presented to her as a gift. She pulled over and threw the whole load into the back seat, and then headed to Sue's workplace, Bonner Garden in the Santa Catalina foothills. The Catalinas bordered Tucson to the north, and the Rincons, where Shandley Gardens was located, were on the far east side. The two gardens were nearly an hour drive from each other, and there were other differences. Bonner had been a public garden for fifty years, and it had a decent endowment and several beneficent donors, none of whom also donated to Shandley. Their director *did* have a "pedigree" from an East Coast botanical garden administration program. But the staffs of both places got along well. People seemed to help each other out in this field.

When Sue got into the car, Bea managed to steer the conversation away from the death of her board member towards who might be the new director at the big Phoenix garden that was hosting the meeting and, of course, to the anticipated start of the monsoon season. The clouds were getting bigger and darker. The winds were already buffeting her little car. A dust devil was gathering force west of the interstate. Luckily it was heading away from the freeway towards the fallow fields.

Sue said, "You know, when I was in elementary school, I learned that Arizona was all about cotton, copper and cattle. But look at what's happened to cotton. How many people do you know who buy one-hundred-percent cotton anymore? It's all synthetics. So now we have these fallow fields and dust storms."

"Well, it's not like it was ever sustainable. It takes so much water. I know a cotton farmer who said he'd never grow the stuff, if he didn't get such high government subsidies."

"Well, so what would you put here? More houses?" Sue

asked.

"God, no. How about growing something that takes less water?" Bea turned to Sue to emphasize her point, then realized she was drifting towards the other lane.

"That could be a big financial risk, if there's no market for it," Sue said, as Bea corrected her path.

"Well, I'm no expert on the economics of it, but there needs to be some kind of cover crop. These dust storms are getting scary. I used to have to pull off the road to wait for one maybe once a season. Now it's almost every time I drive through in June, July and August. Have you looked at old pictures of the Great Dust Bowl lately? There's an uncanny similarity." Bea said this while braking for an idiot who'd just passed her and pulled in front with very little distance between them.

"So, do you have naysayers on your board? Climate change is just 'normal variation'?" Sue asked.

"Oh, yeah. I'm not allowed to schedule a climate change class series."

"Okay, enough of all that… let's talk about something positive. Is it going to rain today?"

"No, that would be too good to be true." Bea was definitely ready for some good luck.

* * *

It was a useful meeting. There were representatives of seven public gardens, and they debated how to engage people who would only take twenty seconds to read a sign.

"Whoa, that's old data. These days we're lucky to hold them for half that time," said the woman who had convened the meeting.

Bea was so engaged in the discussion that she managed to forget about the murder. Three o'clock came quickly; they could still miss the Phoenix rush hour. But that, too, was changing. When they hit the freeway, cars were crawling down the sixteen-lane road like desert tortoises.

They'd been enjoying the air conditioning in the Phoenix garden's gorgeous events building. Bea hadn't been watching the weather and wasn't thinking about the chance of a "haboob." Lately, southern Arizona experienced some of these before a rain. What a word. But it was more powerful than "dust storm." *Haboob* came from an Arabic word for wind. These things could be fifty miles wide and almost two miles high. They could obliterate your view of anything, so that day became night.

At first Bea thought the wind wouldn't be that bad. On the interstate heading back south to Tucson she had maybe 300 feet of visibility. But then it got darker, and her little car was walloped by a blast. She was moving into a wall of dust and could see only fifty feet now. She turned on the air conditioning "recirc" button. She strained to see the highway signs, and then she gave up.

"Can you see that sign?" she asked Sue, her shoulders aching from her grip on the steering wheel.

"No. You'd better pull over. My God, it's like the sun just set!"

On other road trips, Bea had been able to read the storm signs on the interstate. They said you were supposed to pull over if there was a dust storm and turn off your lights. She didn't like the part about turning off her lights. She didn't want to do it; what if somebody else decided to pull over right where she was? But she supposed that if somebody saw her lights, they'd drive that way, on the shoulder.

There were dark shapes along the side of the freeway that must be other cars. Okay, maybe people *would* see her. There were little pebbles bouncing off her windshield as she pulled over and stopped. She let out a breath.

They listened to the radio. The Tucson National Public Radio station was telling people to stay off the interstate to Phoenix. Bea's cell phone rang. It was Frank. He was listening to NPR, too.

"Bea, are you O.K.?"

"Not really. It's like midnight with no city lights, and even with the air on recirc we're starting to cough. I think I have at least two new cracks on my windshield from the rocks that keep hitting it. Not to mention the fact that I won't be home when the kids get off the bus. My God, can you hear that noise? Is this what a hurricane sounds like?"

"Sit tight until it blows over. I can meet the bus if you want, too, and I can bring them home to wait for you."

Bea wasn't sure she wanted to tell Frank where the hiding place for her front door key was. She didn't know him that well yet. She wasn't sure she wanted him waiting for her on the couch with her kids, either. It was nice of him, but she just wasn't ready for this kind of intimacy.

Sue was listening to the call. "I can get my husband to meet the bus. That way you can get them when you drop me off. Andy knows my husband from soccer coaching, right?"

This was true. "Thanks, Sue. I'll take you up on it. Hopefully, we'll be back soon."

She told Frank, "Thanks, Frank, but they're taken care of. I'll let you know when I'm home."

"Okay. Be careful, Bea."

"Of course." She hung up. *It's nice to have somebody thinking about you when you're in trouble. I haven't had that for a while. But I'm afraid of letting myself be comfortable with his concern. If you get too comfortable, you can get hurt.* She didn't say it out loud because Sue was deep in conversation with her husband.

They had to sit by the road for two whole hours. Sue's husband called and said he'd bought pizza. The haboob was on national news. The rest of the news on NPR was equally bad, so they listened to music on the community radio station, instead. The car was rattled and pelted, and Bea felt like she was on a small boat in a churning midnight sea.

Finally black air went brown. Cars started up and pulled onto the freeway. Bea took a breath and moved slowly into the right lane. She wouldn't get home for another hour and a half and she was going to need a shoulder rub when she got there. She wondered if Frank was good at that.

She realized she was more than a little inconsistent. She'd just been worrying about being too comfortable with him.

"We're really going to have to do a better job of interpreting climate change at our gardens," Sue said. "With the soil moisture disappearing, there will be a lot more of these things."

Right at this moment, Bea decided it was more important to keep her friends out of jail than to worry about educating people about the effects of climate change. At least it gave her some insight into people who couldn't care less about it. Certain things in one's life took precedence. Feeding your children. Staying alive on the freeway. And keeping your friends out of jail.

But she had to check herself. If this trip to Phoenix, complete with a haboob, had happened just a week ago, her reaction would have been increased frustration at Liz for blocking Bea's attempts at educating people about how Tucson was changing. Was there somebody at Shandley who had been furious enough about this to actually murder Liz?

Bea dropped Sue off at her house in midtown, not far from her own one-story unit at #14 Palo Verde Acres. Sue came home to a brightly lit house and a long hug from her husband, which Bea knew would be quite different from the dark home she'd encounter. But fortunately, Andy seemed relaxed after spending time with his soccer coach, and both children were happy about having pepperoni and sausage pizza, which was not what Bea usually ordered for them.

"Mom, we saw the storm on TV! We were looking for your car!" Andy said as she buckled the kids into their car seats.

"It was probably too dark to see us. It was like the middle of the night with no stars out. Let's go home. I need to eat something!"

Frank called just then. "I've been worried about you. Glad you're okay. Can I at least bring over a pizza?" Pizza seemed to be the theme of the night. Bea could no longer resist. She was so tired and so hungry. She told him yes.

She was reading the kids a book when he showed up with a Veggie Delight large pizza, a chopped salad and some Dos Equis beers. He offered to read a couple more books while she ate.

"I can read. Let me read the next one!' said Andy.

"That's even better," said Frank.

This was turning into quite the domestic scene. Bea could almost relax, and yet... would Frank abandon all of them in a week or two?

Andy had picked a chapter book, which meant he needed help. Jessie got bored by the whole thing and came over to eat a piece of her mother's pizza. She could eat anything any-time. She'd probably be okay no matter what. Andy moved closer to Frank. Frank smiled at him. Andy would be the most hurt of any of them if Frank decided to bail.

Maybe she shouldn't have included him in her home life for two nights in a row. Better to be lonely and exhausted than hurt. Better than Andy getting hurt. One of her col-lege roommates, far more solitary than she was, used to say, "Those workout coaches have it backwards. No gain, no pain." But she could tell that Andy and Jessie didn't want to kick Frank out the door. And she could use the extra help in getting them to bed tonight. She was tired, so tired. What she really wanted was a bathtub soak, except the apartment had no tub. And sleep, she wanted sleep.

After the kids were in bed, Frank asked if she wanted him to massage her shoulders. She didn't mention that she'd thought about this during the haboob.

"Sure, that'd be nice."

"You don't sound so sure about that."

"Sorry." But it turned out he was good at it. He had very strong hands, and he knew about muscles. Maybe he'd learned about that in medical school before he dropped out.

"Why'd you drop out of med school, Frank?"

"It was the competition. I was channeling a side of myself that I don't really like. So now I'm an impoverished writer. Although I did just sell something to *Outdoors Magazine*. A profile of a four-generations-old organic family farm in Virginia."

"Do you regret your decision to leave med school?"

"Not yet. Maybe if I'm successful at this writing business I can give you a more resounding 'no.'"

"Fair enough."

"I can tell you one thing, though. People always say that writing is a lonely business. I don't think I'm as much of an introvert as many writers, so it's been nice to hang out with you and the kids."

"Good." Best to leave it at that.

There was a smidgeon of rain now; Bea watched it make trails through the dust on her windows, and she tried to relax like the droplets falling slowly down...

"Well, we're not getting much this time, but it's raining somewhere," Frank said. He massaged her scalp a bit, and then smoothed her hair down. He left with a gentle kiss on the cheek. And she actually was hoping for a little more. Curious.

Bea let herself review the current state of affairs before she turned to the pruning article that had put her to sleep a few nights before. She'd be returning to the murder pit tomorrow. Ethan would be meeting about the will. Maybe some good could come out of this; maybe Liz had left them lots of money. And maybe Marcia had found some ancient enemy of Liz's who'd tried to do her in, someone unrelated to the Gardens, and Shandley could go on peacefully with the same cast of characters. She sure as hell hoped so.

CHAPTER TEN

The next day she skipped her meditation. In half an hour the Gardens would be open to the public for the first time since Liz's death. And everybody knew it was a murder. No doubt they'd be full of looky-loos wanting to see where the branch had fallen. The whole eucalyptus grove was cordoned off, so nobody could wander around there, supposedly because the Gardens didn't want the liability of another accident. Well, that really *had* been Angus's original reason for doing it.

There was a voicemail from Marcia. "Call me."

When Bea got her on the line, Marcia was full of questions about Dr. Ramos. "Tell me, did you say that your Dr. Ramos is an invasive plants specialist?"

"Well, he's hardly *my* Dr. Ramos. But yeah, that's his area of expertise. Invasive non-native plants, and how climate change can increase them."

"There was a title page of a scientific article in the leaf litter in your eucalyptus grove. It was deep in the litter, so we didn't find it right off. Something about how climate-change induced wildfires are increasing invasive plants in their wake."

"Well, that's something Ramos would read, all right. But why would he take a scientific paper out there when he was going to kill somebody? Couldn't it be a set-up? Or just coincidence?"

"Those are two possibilities. This paper finally has some fingerprints on it, and we are getting Ramos's. Of course, even if they're his, someone could have taken it out of his briefcase."

"He does leave his car unlocked. He opened it once to show me some plants he'd collected."

"So, who would want to set him up? How does Javier feel about him? And Ethan?'

"Marcia, I know there's mutual professional respect there. The bond of plantsmen."

"Maria?"

"I doubt she's ever met him. Maybe somebody is setting them all up, with Maria's mosaics and Ramos's scientific papers."

"And who would you say might do that?"

"I don't know. Myron and Buffy don't like Ramos's politics; they think he's a leftie environmentalist, but why try to get him convicted of murder for politics? And they appreciate Javier's work. Everybody, including Liz, has felt that way. And I don't know if any board members even notice Maria. Except maybe Alicia. You know the syndrome. The part-time, somehow invisible Latina cleaner."

"Yes. So, she could be a convenient scapegoat for someone."

"You're not asking me about Angus."

"No. We haven't dismissed the possibility that either he or Alicia were involved, but they are not the focus of our investigation right now. They came back together from the Events Center site viewing, and they vouch for each other. Okay, Bea. That's it for now. Keep your eyes and ears open." She hung up the phone.

Bea settled in to do actual work, the kind she had been hired for. She made some calls to patio garden tour homeowners, and said yes, of course, the show would go on, and by the time the tour happened (which was only a few days away now), the murder would be cleared up. She filled some more volunteer slots. Ethan walked by her open door, and he didn't look happy. He'd been tense ever since this business started. Since he'd never been a forthcoming guy, she decided to go by his office and see what was up now.

"Hey, boss, you'll be glad to know the patio home tour is coming together. We now have a waiting list. I wish we could increase the size of the tour, but there are those fire marshal's limits for the luncheon at the end in the boardroom..."

"Yes, just another one of the limitations we face for raising money around here."

"That'll change with the Events Center." He shrugged.

This wasn't like Ethan. "I hope nothing else horrible has happened," Bea said.

"Well, Bea, at least no one can say I killed Liz to get her bequest for the Gardens."

"That bad, huh?"

"It's not very polite to complain about a $10,000 bequest. And I am grateful. The funds are to go to garden maintenance, and we all know that's crucial. I guess I'm being such an ingrate because she gave larger gifts to the arts council and her church, according to Myron. And she endowed the symphony with a couple of million bucks.

"And she left millions to Myron?"

"He said she left him 'the balance of her estate.' I don't know how much that is, but... I shouldn't be even be thinking this, much less saying it to you. I guess I thought..."

"You thought the Gardens meant more to her? But it was Alan's thing, right? She sure got rid of the place fast after he died."

"Well, yeah."

"Ethan, do you think–It's horrible to talk this way, but I know we're all thinking like this—because this *does* give Myron a motive."

"I think it's best if you and I don't play amateur detective."

Well, he'd shut *that* window of candor between them. He was back in boss mode. He was probably right, but Marcia had asked her to ferret things out. And Javier seemed to be in trouble, and Marcia hadn't asked her anything about Angus, so that was good, but she figured anything could happen at this point. Until they caught the real murderer.

She took a walk on the grounds to clear her head. The Gardens' grounds didn't have their usual calming effect. There were maybe a hundred people craning their heads at the eucalyptus tree that was cordoned off with a double row of tape, inside the single row that Angus had put around the whole grove.

Bea crossed the big lawn, soon to shrink to make way for the Events Center. There was no denying that the cool green grass was a pleasure. A guilty pleasure. Lawns were good in public spaces where people played ball or picnicked on them, but they could easily get by at Shandley with half an acre of grass instead of three. The roses nearby were looking peaked, and the tulips, of course, had long since bloomed. But the cactus and succulent garden was spectacular, as always. This garden, too, was full of people. It seemed that murder might be increasing their admissions take that day. There was at least *one* positive effect.

The spines and dried fruits of the golden barrel cacti shone yellow in the intense sunlight. And among the columnar cacti, it wasn't just the saguaros that were fruiting; the organ pipes' rosy-yellow tennis-ball sized fruits were splitting open, revealing sweet, red, succulent seedy insides. Alan had brought these back from Mexico, along with a couple of big, fat *cardón* cacti, in the days when importing plants from Mexico was considerably more laissez-faire. Bea watched some tourists reading the "DO NOT TOUCH THE PLANTS" sign she'd installed after a child had stroked the white "beard" of an old man cactus, only to howl in pain at the sharp spines under the beard. A pretty benign plant problem, compared to sawed off eucalyptus branches.

It seemed Bea was never going to be able to let her mind get far from the damned murder. Myron was walking the grounds, too. *Watch out, you might get some sun!* she thought unkindly. He looked remarkably hale and hearty, for Myron. She nodded as they passed near the tropical greenhouse.

Bea opened the greenhouse door to humidity and the rich smell of decaying plants. Tucsonans called monsoon season *humid*. People from Georgia laughed at that, and who knew what people from rainforests would say. Plants decayed in smell-free anonymity in the desert, but not so in this little corner of the Gardens. There was a sprinkler system in the building (more water), but once again, the specimens were glorious. Alan had done a lot of orchid collecting in Mexico and Central America in his youth. There were some orchids in bloom at most any time; pink and purple blooms hung from pots and nestled in the crooks of cacao trees.

Bea was attracted by a lovely sweet-scented white ginger flower, when she noticed that there was somebody else in the greenhouse. Buffy was sitting on the little stone bench, looking mournful. She didn't see Bea at first, didn't even notice that Bea had opened the door. She seemed to have shrunk. Her face sagged and Bea suddenly saw her as a too-thin old person, not a poster child for cosmetic surgery. Bea greeted her and Buffy shook her head, as if to throw out her thoughts. About her friend's death? Her lips whipped up into a smile without a trace of joy. "Bea, dear, you surprised me!"

"Sorry." She fit well into the landscape of the tropical greenhouse. Buffy wasn't much bigger than some of the anthuriums there, and her deep tan and bright pink polo shirt and green shorts and sneakers fit the color scheme. Bea had an insight. "Is this one of your favorite places at Shandley?"

"Oh, yes, dear, oh, yes." The second "yes" was said with a startling amount of certainty.

"Well, enjoy it, then." Bea headed for *her* favorite garden, the Sonoran Desert natives area. This garden looked a lot like the wild desert near it, except that Alan and Javier had massed similar plants together, creating beautiful swathes of spiky ocotillos and bendy red limberbushes, and areas seeded so carefully with wildflowers that the spring and post-monsoon blooms made the native plant garden everyone's favorite spot at those times of year. There wasn't much in flower now though, and there wasn't much shade. The green-barked palo verde trees might shield somebody Jessie's size, or a coyote or a cottontail, but not an adult—not even Bea at only 5'2". Alan Shandley had long ago built a lovely stone-and-wood shade ramada in the center of this area. Bea sat down there to think things through.

She was not fated to concentrate, however. A family of

French tourists with kids about Andy and Jessie's age joined her as soon as she sat down. The kids were as whiny as hers would be if she'd dragged them on a hike when it was ninety-five degrees. Bea told them where the nearest drinking fountain was and made what she hoped was a polite exit. She was headed back to her office when Angus stopped her, on the patio off the boardroom. It was just four days ago that she'd watched him tell Ethan about Liz's fall on this same brick patio.

"Hey, I hear you may not go to jail after all! You're not a 'focus' of the investigation!" she told him.

"Bea, until this gets solved, I'm not taking anything for granted."

"Okay, what do you think, Angus? Maybe we can figure it out together."

"Well, I've been noticing some weird stuff."

Bea put her hands out as if to say, "Give it to me."

"Myron's awfully happy for a guy whose mom has been murdered. Although I admit she henpecked him, but still. Ethan's jumpy. Too jumpy. I've never seen him lose his cool like this." When she raised her eyebrows, he said, "Yeah, I know, it's bad when somebody in your inner circle murders your founder. I feel like a traitor saying that. So. There's Buffy. She's wasting away with grief, it seems. And Armando. He's just well—Bea, this is not a word I use, but he's just—*inappropriate*."

"What exactly do you mean? Dr. Ramos is inappropriate a lot."

"Well, he's all excited about replacing Liz on the board, if you can believe it. He says he has several candidates that can make the place governed by 'people who actually know something about plants' and 'people who understand that the world is warming, people who aren't stuck in the last century.' He told me that if even one of these people gets on the board, there will be a three to two majority that's 'reasonable.' I guess he gives Alicia credit for being reasonable. And he says he'd love to get even more of his reasonable people on. The by-laws say we can have up to nine board members, you know."

"Besides the ethical issues, it's kind of stupid to piss off Myron and Buffy right now. They have money and a connection to the Gardens and want to support us. But he'll be disappointed about the endowment that Liz was supposed to leave us. Ethan told me it's not in her will."

"I never thought she'd do that, even if Armando and Ethan did. But really, Bea, everybody around here's becoming unhinged. Javier's a wreck since they searched his house. He called Maria and told her to stay in Mexico."

"That's a good idea. I wish I'd scheduled a vacation this week."

"No, you're our big hope. Don't let the wrong person get nailed for this."

Bea was feeling her responsibilities anew when she got back to her office door, sweaty from a short walk at a normal pace, but she told herself the monsoons *would* come and bring blessed relief from the heat, and this awful suspicion about everybody around her *would* come to an end. Her first reaction, though, when she saw that it was Marcia calling on her cell phone, was dread.

"Hey, Bea." Bea pictured her with a serious, sort of quizzical expression. As if she was trying to decide to break some bad news.

"Tell me a little more about Ethan. How'd he get this job?"

"Well, I don't know. I wasn't here then. Liz, Myron and Buffy hired him. He wasn't in the botanical garden world, he was a nurseryman. Well thought of around here. Knows a lot about native plants. He was up in Phoenix, at a big nursery up there. Manager, native plants expert. I guess they were looking for a plantsman, not necessarily somebody with a botanical gardens background. And I know they didn't pay much in the beginning. They still don't, really."

"So why do you think he left the nursery?"

"Well, I don't know. I expect he considered it a real opportunity to direct a new garden. Why are you asking me all these questions?"

"I'm just wondering if your board knew he had a police

record. Felony. He did some time for possession of a dangerous drug. Interesting that they would overlook that. But maybe, good for them."

"Marcia, I don't know anything about this. You'd better ask Buffy and Myron. I don't know Ethan well, because he keeps his cards very close to his chest. But Marcia, even if he had a drug problem, what does that have to do with murdering Liz?"

"Bea, we'll leave it at that. I realize this is your boss we're talking about, and that puts you in an uncomfortable position."

That was an understatement. Marcia ended with "Ramos's fingerprints match those on the paper we found in the leaf litter. As we discussed, this could be a set-up... or not."

When Bea hung up, she sat in her chair and couldn't think what to do next. Not work, that was for sure. She decided to find Angus to talk about Ethan. Angus was as shocked as she was.

"I wonder if he lied on his job application? I mean, didn't you have to fill out something asking if you'd ever been convicted of a felony?"

"Yeah. So, Marcia will surely get that application, if she doesn't already have it. If he lied about a felony, who knows what else he's lied about?"

* * *

There was nothing good about this day. Bea got a call from Andy's camp director. Actually, the call was for "Mrs. Flynn," and the volunteer answering the phone had initially told him there was no such person. Flynn was Pat, Andy and Jessie's last name; Bea had never changed her name from Rivers, but neither her volunteer nor the camp director knew the complexities of her family's surnames. The camp director had insisted that Andy Flynn's mother had listed Shandley as her place of employment, and the volunteer had put the call through to Bea.

Apparently, some kids had been teasing Andy about

his mom working in a place where people died from falling trees. One boy had taunted him with "Maybe your mom will get hurt, and die, too!" and Andy had punched him hard. At any rate, the kid had to go to the nurse and then home. More violence in Bea's life. This was so atypical of Andy; she'd have to ask Pat if he'd been giving his son self-defense lessons. The camp director admitted that Andy had been bullied, but she asked Bea to reinforce the message that violence was not the way to deal with taunts. Bea said she'd discuss this with Andy and she hoped the school would discuss bullying, so this kind of thing was nipped in the bud.

She didn't have the heart to do much more than hug her son when he got off the bus. He had been crying, and he started up again as she hugged him.

"I'm really sorry, but I'm really worried about you, Mom," he said.

"Don't be," she said. "I'm perfectly safe. And you are, too."

By dinnertime Andy had made a good enough recovery to get on her case for tossing the honey bottle in the garbage instead of washing it out and putting it in the recycling. Bea certainly hoped all the talk about kids being "resilient" was true. At any rate, she expected her son would grow up to be a more charming environmentalist than Armando Ramos.

They ate brown rice and vegetables, and Bea had let them each choose what they wanted to marinate their tofu in. Andy chose honey and water, so Jessie picked something different... chocolate milk. They both professed themselves happy with their chosen dinners. Everybody was calm enough at dinner to talk about how Andy might have reacted differently. Andy decided he would have said, "Eucalyptus branches fall all the time. One fell right in front of Bobby's dog." Since this was true, and Bobby was a friend of the bully, he thought that would have shut the kid up.

After she'd tucked the kids in, she thought about calling Pat about the incident, but she just didn't want to deal with him tonight. Instead, she called Frank.

"Well, good for Andy, but good for you, too." Not what Pat would have said; as far as he was concerned, she did nothing right lately.

"You remembered that I'm going to see my mother in Virginia tomorrow, right?"

"Yeah."

So, I'm going to see what my mother knows about Buffy and Liz."

"Remember not to let her know about the murder."

"I will. Try to have a relaxing weekend, Bea."

"It's a little hard when Marcia calls me in with one revelation after another, but thanks."

CHAPTER ELEVEN

On Friday morning Bea opened her computer to several emails from volunteers. They wanted the inside scoop on the murder. She was trying to decide how to answer them when she had a more immediate concern. Dr. Madsden, the retired plant sciences professor who'd taught that Saturday class just a few days before, plunked down in the chair in front of her desk. Joan Madsden never beat around the bush. She demanded, "What the hell is going on around here, Bea?"

"I wish I knew. The best thing you can do right now is say the police are working on it. *Please* quash any nasty rumors, if you can."

Dr. Madsden leaned forward and brushed her gray bangs out of her eyes. "I am not superhuman, Bea. I love my fellow volunteers, but I *have* noticed that rumors sprout wings even when the topic is less juicy than murder."

Bea was starting to feel desperate about how long this investigation might take. She'd already been wondering how long *she* was going to be able to bear it, and now she was seriously concerned about how long Shandley's decent reputation would hold up. Dr. Madsden read her mind. "Don't worry about Shandley. All kinds of people know about it today who'd never heard of it a couple of days ago. It'll help your bottom line. Shandley's reputation is the least of your worries. I just hope somebody we know here isn't a closet psychopath."

"That's pretty stark. I hadn't thought of it quite that way." *Although I've come pretty close.*

"Sorry. I'll leave you to your work."

Bea shut her door and tried to work. At one point, she looked away from her computer, letting her eyes rest on the mesquite trees framing her window. Behind them, Armando Ramos was leading a university class. He looked trim in his khakis and short–sleeved shirt with a pencil and a pen in the pocket. He had the bushy beard she'd noticed on lots of field biologists. Bea couldn't hear what he was saying—the windows were shut tight to contain the air conditioning—but he was picking up a bean to expound upon the wonders of mesquite as a low-water-use crop, she suspected. She, too, was excited that people were starting to buy mesquite flour in specialty stores and co-ops; this could be an important new crop for arid lands. Maybe Shandley could sell mesquite products in a gift shop someday.

She watched as an eager female student asked a question and then quickly dropped her head. Bea switched her gaze to Ramos's face, which had changed from expository to mocking. She could imagine him saying "absurd," which was one of his favorite words. He actually rolled his eyes at the poor student. Bea wished the guy was a more charismatic crusader for climate change and environmental issues. Even his students probably disliked him.

* * *

At lunchtime Bea managed to get to the public pool. A half hour of a good unbroken breaststroke did wonders for her mood, as it always did. Bea cherished these moments, the only time in her week when she wasn't responsible for other people: kids, volunteers, now, for God's sake, for making sure good people stayed out of jail. All she had to do in the pool was turn around when she got to the edge. Motion, water, arms, legs, cool water, bright sun, empty mind.

Back at work, her tension had dissipated enough that she welcomed Angus when he knocked at the door. Two raps, space, two raps.

"Come on in, Angus."

"Bea, I have to talk this over with you. I just heard a really weird conversation."

"Has there been a conversation that isn't weird since all this started?"

"I wasn't really trying to eavesdrop. I was heading in to talk to Ethan, but he was in there with Armando. The door was part-way open. I was going to move on, but they were shouting. So, I stood in the hall like a little kid listening in on his parents' fight."

"I've never heard them fighting."

"And you've never heard Ethan get emotional, either. But trust me, he was hardly the soul of patience."

"For God's sake don't keep me in suspense."

"It looks like Armando hasn't made a lot of friends in academia. He told Ethan he was almost certain he wasn't going to get tenure. I didn't know he didn't have it... I thought he was maybe fifty. But what do I know about stuff like that? He was saying he didn't relish living in East Podunk, New Mexico or, worse yet, Iowa, where he's been applying for jobs. He doesn't want to leave the Sonoran Desert. But he told Ethan that he could be a great 'curator of plants' at Shandley, and we could be a 'cutting edge research garden' and test out all kinds of plant adaptations to climate change, and we could have a 'fantastic climate-change education program'... I figured you'd like that part."

"Ethan yelled at him for that?"

"No, not yet. He just told Armando that we can't even support the staff we have, much less a Ph.D. curator. Then Armando said that even though Liz didn't endow the Gardens, Buffy could, she was a helluva lot more interested in plants than Liz ever was. He started talking about that guy Buffy brought in to 'educate' the board."

"You mean that guy that was trying to get all our board members to take out an insurance policy naming the Gardens? That guy who gave everybody 'actuarial tables' to show when they'd die?" Bea had found this move absolutely incredible. She remembered that the older board members looked quite shaken at what the table called their "projected death dates," which the expert had at least not mentioned out loud.

"Yeah, that was weird, all right. But Armando thought that since Buffy brought him in, she was interested in long-term big-money contributions to the Gardens. And that she'd provide for us, beyond the Events Center. So, when he told Ethan that, Ethan got pissed. He said that if Armando was expecting Buffy to endow his position, he'd need to be a little more respectful of her. And of everyone there. And that at this point, we all needed to do everything we could to help the police solve this murder investigation, so that we could get back to the business of planning to keep what we have afloat, much less expanding. I'm surprised you didn't hear him all the way over here in your office. This murder has sure gotten under his skin."

"Well, yeah. It hasn't gotten under yours? I just hope Buffy follows through on the Events Center donation after her best friend got killed. I think Dr. Ramos is crazy to think she'll do more than that. Does he think this scheme of his is going to actually increase our visitors and bring in money here?"

"I don't think Armando thinks like that at all. But he probably has thought that getting his buddies on the board would help him get hired."

"Exactly."

It seemed absurd to think that bumping off Liz would help Dr. R.'s career plans. Well, one thing she realized from reading stories of people's crimes was that they often had their own private logic, which bore no resemblance to common sense most of the time. Things didn't have to make sense to *her*; they needed to make sense to the murderer.

* * *

She got through the day and spent a blessedly uneventful Friday night with her two kids, watching a DVD of *101 Dalmatians* that her mother had given them.

Right on schedule, after they were in bed, Pat called.

"Bea, I have to cancel taking the kids tomorrow."

"Of course you do. What's your back-up plan?"

"Don't you know somebody who can take them? I'll be

able to take them next Saturday, but I have an important business meeting."

This brought to mind the last "important business meeting" he'd had, requiring her to change her plans. Barb and John Rice had seen him at one of Tucson's finest restaurants with a very attractive woman. Barb reported that the business they were conducting "wasn't exactly professional."

The bottom line was that the kids were 100% her responsibility, except when Pat chose to find times compatible with his social life. She had to respond. She'd try to keep it reasonable. If she got emotional, that just meant she couldn't be dealt with. That was their pattern.

"Pat, you said you'd go to Andy's soccer game. It's important to him. And I really need to go to Liz Shandley's memorial service."

"*I* need to go to this meeting. Things come up. I need to take care of them to have enough money to, among other things, pay you child support. Can't you ask Barb Rice? She doesn't work, right?"

"It's Saturday tomorrow, Pat. Supposedly, you're not working, either. Here's the thing: is your business meeting more important than me going to a memorial service that's part of *my* work? When we'd agreed that you'd take the kids? What's your business meeting about?"

"None of your business."

"It's hard to trust you, when people have seen you on dates in nice restaurants when you told me you had a business meeting." She took a breath. It was getting hard to stay calm.

"That's entirely inappropriate of you, Bea. The bottom line is that my business meetings bring in money, and yours won't yield us anything."

"There's more to being a parent than providing child support, Pat."

"I have to go," he said. "Next weekend for sure." And he hung up.

It's all up to me, as usual. I wish I made enough money not to take another penny from him. But I'll continue to take it, because he owes it to me, according to the courts. Because the kids need it, damn it.

Bea kicked Jessie's bunny across the room, imagining kicking Pat in the shins. She paced between the kitchen and the living room, until she knew what she'd do. Andy needed a parent at his game. She needed to go to the memorial service. Barb's son was on Andy's soccer team; Bea could take Andy and Jessie to the game, and then Barb could bring the kids home with her while Bea went to the memorial service around half time.

She called Barb and broached the plan. Her dear friend told her to take all the time she needed. Barb, who Pat said didn't "work," was stepping into the breach once again, taking care of four kids instead of two. She'd tell Pat he ought to have the Rice kids over.

Bea banged through her drawers looking for what to wear the next day. Her soccer team tee shirt and jeans. And for the memorial service? She went to the closet and hunted. She pulled out the flouncy red skirt she'd bought for dancing with Pat and put it in a Salvation Army bag she kept in the hall closet. She plopped down on the hall floor and thought about how she'd gotten involved with the guy.

Pat was a smooth talker and an even smoother dancer. Tall, svelte, graceful, red-haired like Andy, green-eyed. He'd swept Bea off her feet, literally and figuratively. And he'd started out as a committed environmentalist, marketing green cleaning products. They'd had good times together, rafting the Colorado River, hiking the Sierra Nevada, and dancing everywhere from ballrooms to back country bars. But once the kids were born, the drudgery of childcare conflicted with the life Pat wanted to lead, especially as he rose in the business world. Bea's Earth Mother style—those cotton shifts, stone earrings, and Birkenstocks—most certainly did *not* comport with the Chamber of Commerce wife her husband wanted her to become. So, he'd found another woman who fit his image better. Of course, *that* relationship hadn't lasted long after the divorce, which gave Bea some solace.

It was interesting to see the "green products" businessman driving a big SUV now. Black, no less. Tucsonans usually avoided black because it heated up the interior immediately. Andy gave his dad a hard time about his "carbon footprint." She hadn't taught him about that; he was only seven, for goodness sake, but he'd picked it up somewhere, probably from his enviro second grade teacher.

Pat was planning to take the kids to his mother's for a week in August… at least that week was taken care of on the calendar. She thought the trip would happen, mostly because Pat's mother in Oregon loved having the kids visit. Not much else about her ex-husband's childcare was certain. If there ever was a next time around, Bea would be looking for somebody solid, dancing be damned.

Bea pulled the blouse she'd usually worn with her dancing skirt off the hanger and put it in the Salvation Army bag. Also her ballet slippers. If she ever went dancing with anybody else, she'd wear jeans and sneakers.

Her eyes fell on a book of desert poems that she'd recommended to Frank. She didn't even know if he liked to dance. He wasn't graceful. She pictured his stocky physique and she suddenly wanted the comfort of his voice. It wasn't that late, and he was something of a night owl. Well, it was late in Virginia where he was now, but she had his cell number, and surely it wouldn't wake his mother up. She called him.

He sounded half-strangled when he answered, and she was about to ask if he was all right, but she knew his problem even before she heard a woman's voice in the background, saying "Frank," in a horribly intimate way. It was not an old woman's voice. Who knew if Frank really even had a mother in Virginia? She'd probably been a complete fool about this just like she'd been in expecting Pat to be a good parent. Or in thinking her colleagues were blameless. She hung up.

Watching the kids sleep was no soporific for her that night, and neither wine nor herb tea was any help either.

CHAPTER TWELVE

Bea had settled on her black cotton shift and black sandals for the memorial service. The outfit would have to do. It was Tucson in summer—it would do. She was in charge of her life, her job, and her kids, and she needed to make her own rules. She'd just have to change in the bathroom at the ballpark.

"You really can't stay for the whole game?" Andy asked.

"Almost the whole game, honey. I just have to duck out for the last few minutes."

"Well, okay." He pulled his ear.

"Andy, believe me, I'd rather watch you than go to this. But I feel like it might help me figure out who killed Mrs. Shandley. And it would be good for our whole family if I figured this out. When I pick you up from Barb's we'll all get some ice cream."

"Yippee!" Jessie yelled.

"Okay," Andy said. She hoped it was.

On the way to the park, there seemed to be a sound system in the car that kept playing that low-pitched, sexy woman's voice pleading, "Frank." Bea was as bad at banishing that sound as she was at dispelling the images of Liz's mosaics. But she was trying, and damn it, she would keep trying.

Andy played goalie, and he did a fine job of blocking some plays. Jessie, Barb, and Bea all screamed like crazy when he made a good play, and he was looking happy with himself when Bea had to make her bathroom change. He did frown, though, when he saw her wave goodbye. God damn Pat for putting her in this position.

She checked herself in the car mirror as she sped to the

church. She was wearing only one earring. She pulled out the silver hoop as she nearly ran to the church door. The usher moved to the door as if he wanted to bar her entry. She gave him a solemn look and slowed her pace to a respectful walk. His expression brightened and he handed her an order of service.

She had to wait until the opening prayer was over before she slid into a pew next to Angus and Javier, who were saving her a place. After the eulogy, the Symphony Director would say a few words, in addition to Buffy and Ethan.

The huge church was packed. Ethan was sitting up front with Myron and Buffy and a couple of older people. Maybe Liz's relatives from the East? Both men wore well-fitting dark suits. Myron was an older, paler, more flaccid version of Ethan, but they both looked like men "of substance" in those fine suits on either side of Buffy. She, on the other hand, was just a thin swatch of purple silk between their presences… *she* wasn't hung up on wearing black, it seemed.

Alicia and Raoul Vargas were in the second row, in a big cluster of people that Bea recognized as key members of Tucson's business and political community. The second row looked a whole lot less lonely than the first row. But after all, Alicia's family had been members of Tucson's business class longer than most of the Anglos in the audience. As had Raoul's, in Mexico. That counted for something in Tucson, thank goodness.

Armando Ramos came in just as the priest was starting his eulogy and sat in the back row pew.

The priest went on about what a model wife and mother Liz was, and how she had contributed so much to her community. Her generosity had "opened stunning gardens, the product of years of her husband's love and care, to the public." She had also helped to make the Tucson Symphony "a jewel in our crown."

He went through her life: born "in comfort" in New York. He acknowledged the presence of her brother and sister-in-law from New York. They must be the folks sitting in the front pew with Buffy, Myron, and Ethan, and the well-dressed woman who must be the Symphony Director. The priest mentioned the Davenport School, "which our dear friend Mrs. Buffy Jones will tell us about." Then on to Blanchard College in Boston, where Liz met "the love of her life," Alan Shandley, who was an up-and-coming Harvard boy. After a few years in the East, they moved to Tucson, to "make their fortunes," and "begin their admirable history of community service." A long list of boards followed. Alan had not shirked his nonprofit duties, and Liz became prominent on boards as his career took off. "Their dear son Myron, born in Tucson, has followed in his father's footsteps, continuing his real estate business and sitting on several community boards, including that of Shandley Gardens." Bea looked over at Myron. His shoulders suddenly tensed inwards.

Buffy was up next. The fine bones in her face were too prominent. Her eyes were puffy. But the purple silk suit matched her silk-covered pumps, and the simple gold jewelry was utterly tasteful. It matched the gold highlights in her short bob.

"It's difficult for me to stand up here today. But I want to talk about a memory of Liz. It takes place a long time ago, when we were sophomores at the Davenport School, in Virginia. That memory symbolizes what was best between us, and what was best about Liz.

"We were playing field hockey. She was a wing, and I was a forward. She was fast. She would get the ball and carry it all the way up the field and send it to me. And I would shoot for the goal and make it, or not, but I couldn't do it without Liz, and she couldn't do it without me, and we were famous for making goals, together. It wasn't about me, it wasn't about her, it wasn't about *anyone else,* it was about that amazing fusion that can only happen when two people care about and understand each other. I so mourn that today."

The congregation was silent in a way they hadn't been after the priest's platitudes.

The Symphony President, Mrs. John Pierce III, was next. Her thick auburn hair framed a pinched face with small eyes and lips. She wore a simple black sheath and a strand of pearls over a slim, busty body. She kept talking about "my dear friend Liz," but it wasn't clear if their friendship extended beyond "Liz's extraordinary generosity and community spirit" in providing funds that allowed the symphony to bring in its current "world class" conductor, "putting Tucson on the world stage." Bea tried to see Ethan's face, but all she could see was the back of his head.

He was the next speaker. His expression was serious, respectful, completely appropriate, of course. His black suit fitted him well. His tie was understated, with dark blue and green stripes. If she hadn't known otherwise, she would have taken him for a young lawyer. "I have always loved plants. Some might say that I loved them more than people. I enjoyed connecting people with the right plants for their lives, for their environment, when I was in the nursery trade. But I owe it to Liz, and her son Myron, and her friend Buffy, for affording me the opportunity to do more than sell plants. Alan Shandley created a place that could inspire people in a way that I never could as a nurseryman. I am able to do something—we're not there yet, but we will get there—of great value in this complicated and sometimes dispiriting world. Liz Shandley gave her home for this to happen. She will always be remembered for this."

His voice cracked a little. She'd never seen this side of him. And yesterday he had yelled at Dr. Ramos. The earth seemed to have gone into a new orbit.

They recited the 23rd psalm together and sang a hymn that Bea had never heard about angels and paradise. The priest mentioned that all were welcome at a reception at a nearby hotel. And then they filed outside the church. The Shandley staff huddled in the shade of a nearby palo verde. Bea moved closer to Angus as Armando appeared behind her.

"Are you guys going to the reception?" he asked. "Myron's hosting it with his Uncle Alfred from New York. Nice location. No church basement for them."

"I don't think so," Angus said.

"Probably not," Bea said.

"No," Javier added.

"Suit yourselves. I think it's important politically." Armando said with a shrug and moved towards the parking lot.

"Where does that guy get off, Angus? Now does he think he can get Uncle Alfred to fund an endowment for him?" Bea asked.

"I don't know, Bea. But I know I'm not going," he responded.

Bea shook her head. "It's just too much right now. And I've promised Andy and Jessie some ice cream."

"I doubt I'm welcome. Besides, I met 'Uncle Alfred' once." Javier said. He waved goodbye to them both.

"What on earth did *that* mean? Is this a class thing or... what do you think he meant, Angus?"

"Well, I don't think he ever felt comfortable with anybody in the Shandley family except Alan. And Myron doesn't like him."

"I never noticed that."

"Javier once told me that Alan Shandley used to bug his son about being more interested in the outdoors, 'like Javier is.' Myron doesn't care one whit about gardening, as far as I can tell. Or about real estate. And Alan was kind of macho, by all accounts. Myron didn't measure up. Javier did. And unlike some of his associates around here," Angus widened his eyes, "Alan wasn't racist. So, there's probably a lot there. Myron is probably jealous of Javier at some basic level."

"Yeah, well he got the inheritance. It's him throwing the party with Uncle Alfred. I don't think Myron has any reason to complain about Javier now."

"Well, Bea, human beings don't make a lot of sense sometimes," Angus said.

"Funny, I was just thinking that earlier."

Buffy had come up to them during the last part of their conversation.

"What are you two looking so conspiratorial about?" she asked.

"Oh, it's nothing, Buffy, just some theory of Angus's."

"Well, Angus, could this be a theory about who did Liz in?"

"I wish I knew, ma'am." Angus couldn't handle calling her by her first name. "I sure wish I knew." He raised an eyebrow at Bea and took off for the parking lot.

"I just don't think I'm up to another big gathering right now. I have to have dinner with the Shandley family tonight, anyway." Buffy said this looking off a little to the side, where Myron was vigorously shaking hands with well-wishers, next to his uncle, a distinguished gentleman with a walrus mustache, and Mrs. Uncle Alfred, who looked like she would rather be in Boston. Armando Ramos was trying to engage her in earnest conversation.

Buffy swung her head back and looked right at Bea. "Bea, dear, would you care to come over for a cup of tea? It would be restorative, and I believe your company would as well."

Well, this is astounding. Buffy had certainly never asked her over before. She'd never really paid much attention to Bea. She was curious, and curiously complimented. Barb had told her to take her time. Okay, she'd go. She supposedly worked part of Saturdays, anyway, and this was work. And even if it wasn't, it was time for her to do what she could to get this thing solved. Marcia was relying on her, and her colleagues were, too. And what she'd said to Andy and Jessie was also true. The sooner this was solved, the better it would be for their little family.

But she'd already missed the end of the soccer game, and there was that promise of ice cream. Damn it. And damn Frank Ferguson for making her life even messier.

"Buffy, what a nice invitation. I guess I'm not sure where you live, though."

It turned out that Buffy lived over in the Rincon Mountain foothills, not far from Shandley. Bea took her time driving over there, so Buffy wouldn't feel rushed.

The house was set back on a long driveway in a grove of mature mesquite trees, a mesquite "bosque," along Rincon Creek. An ocotillo fence marked one boundary. These were called "living fences," because some of the long, thorny canes could root and sprout leaves when it rained. Buffy's fence had been there awhile; a couple of the canes had actually grown beyond the top of the fence line. If it ever rained this summer, maybe these ocotillos would even sport the long red tubular flowers hummingbirds loved.

The front gate was a masterful piece of iron artwork, full of the flora and fauna of the Sonoran desert. There were packs of javelinas, the wild pig-like mammals common in the Rincons. A couple of coyotes howled, minus the red bandannas the tourist traps seemed to feel they needed. They were surrounded by saguaros, ocotillos, and prickly pear cactus. Bea thought it was odd that the front gate was open. No wonder someone had been able to leave the mosaic on Buffy's porch. She resolved to ask Buffy about this.

The gate opened into a courtyard filled with pots. Buffy had chosen beautiful Mexican urns painted with yellow, green, red, and blue flowers to match the flowered Mexican tiles arching over her front door. The shady parts of the patio under mesquites had pots and the sunny parts did, too. There were herbs—basil, oregano, thyme—in one corner, and African "desert roses" with their thick succulent stems in another. And in a third, Bea recognized some Sonoran Desert perennials that were dormant for now. It looked like Buffy also had her own small tropical greenhouse... she glimpsed what looked like orchids through the glass.

"Yes, I can't live without tropicals," said Buffy, who had opened the door as Bea was looking around the corner. "Come in, my dear." She led Bea through a hall with several fine pieces of Western Art in huge gold-gilt frames. There were cowboys watering their horses at sunset, cowboys braving a snowstorm in high mountains, and cowboys sharing coffee with a Navajo, framed by the red sandstone buttes of Monument Valley. Javier had called this "cowboy and Indian" stuff, and said that Liz had taken all of the Shandleys' to town with her.

They came into a huge living room with picture windows that faced the patio garden. The living room ceiling was held up with pine beams interspersed with saguaro ribs.

There were some very fine Navajo rugs on the walls. Two Grey Hills, if she was not mistaken; the weavers used natural wools and wove geometric patterns with grey, brown, cream, beige, black. Sliding glass doors at the back of the room led out to an expanse of lawn and a small rose garden. She could see into the dining room, which was not separated by a wall. A beautiful long table of mahogany, probably, had just one linen place mat and a formal setting at the far end. There was a jigsaw puzzle in the middle. Family oil portraits hung on the walls. Both of the men had severe expressions and gold watch chains. Both of the women had high collars and tight bodices and looked miserable. Barb would tell her she was "projecting" about that.

Buffy noticed that she'd stopped at the dining room door. "Yes, that's the family, for better or for worse. I do feel that they're monitoring my actions, sometimes."

"I can see how you'd feel that." So much so, Bea thought, that she'd take "the family" off the wall. And put them where?

"I guess you can't exactly put them out in the garage."

"No, they wouldn't be comfortable out there at all. Nor would my relatives, if they ever found them out there. My family is inordinately proud of being Mayflower types. And inordinately disapproving of the Western life I chose to live."

Buffy led her to a smaller table and chairs in the living room. Like the cabinet nearby, they were made from carved mesquite. If the dining room bespoke Buffy's East Coast past, the living room was all about the Southwest. Except for the tea service; Buffy had set out a little silver teapot and white china cups with saucers on the mesquite table. The silver sugar bowl had a tiny spoon, and the white china cream pitcher was of the same dainty stuff as the cups. Bea was used to drinking tea out of large mismatched mugs. She felt like one of her mugs as she looked over at the older woman, still wearing her deep purple silk suit and matching silk-covered pumps, with a white silk blouse and a gold choker and earrings delicate enough for her small, thin figure. But Buffy surprised her by complimenting her on her Navajo sandcast bracelet. "What a lovely piece of jewelry, Bea."

Really, why was she so fazed by this woman's elegance? Wasn't she old enough to feel comfortable in her own skin?

Buffy poured her some tea; yes, she'd love some half-and half, no sugar. Buffy took hers "straight up," as she called it.

"This must be a very difficult time for you, Buffy." *Now I'm the one spouting platitudes.*

"More than you know, my dear, more than you know." This was said as she looked at one of her paintings, not at Bea. Bea glanced at the painting. It didn't say anything to her: a group of men and women on horseback among a prolific stand of saguaros. Buffy turned to face her. "But let's talk about you."

Bea wasn't sure why they should talk about her, nor why Buffy felt the need to simulate what was obviously a false cheeriness, but, hey, she'd oblige. Maybe she'd figure something out about Buffy this way.

"You have children, don't you, dear?"

"I have two. Andy is seven. He's a sweet little boy, although maybe too sensitive for his own good, especially given my recent divorce. My five-year-old girl is energetic, saucy, able to let things roll off her back."

"You're lucky, Bea. No husband and two children. I love children, and I was not able to have them. And marriage, as you know, can be a trial."

"Well, yes, I do know that." *Dating's not so easy either, these days.* She tried another tack. "But... it seems you also love gardening."

"Oh, yes. Although there's more here than I can take care of by myself. You know, in the old days, Javier took care of our place, too. But Alan collected so many plants Javier had to be there full time. So, I've had a gardener three days a week. This last one was the best. Pedro helped with everything. I can barely do the weeding anymore, much less the tree trimming." She sighed. "But now Pedro's gone back to Chiapas. He doesn't want his wife and daughters to risk the border crossing, so he's gone home. I gave him a good going-away gift, and I hope they can make a living there. My garden doesn't show his absence... *yet.*"

Bea wasn't sure where to take the conversation from there. Buffy seemed so lonely, and Bea wanted to establish some connection between them before she started asking questions that might help with the murder. She tried to channel Marcia. What would *she* ask? But then Buffy came to the point.

"Bea, the detective working on this wretched murder is an old friend of yours, is that right?"

Of course, this is why she invited me to her home, Bea thought. Aloud, she said, "Well, yes, we went to high school together."

"Is she getting any closer to closure on this awful case?"

"Buffy, I honestly don't know. She manages to ask me a lot more than she tells me."

Buffy was examining her hands. The veins stood out among the liver spots, a whole landscape. Bea had to remember to wear more sunscreen. Suddenly Buffy looked up. "Do *you* have any theories, my dear?"

"Not really." She was not going to get baited into something she'd regret.

"Would you indulge me in hearing a few of my thoughts?"

"Please do."

"Well, as the media keeps mentioning, Alicia and Raoul Vargas had good reason to hate Liz. I don't think the media has even discovered some of the old fights. But I really can't see why murdering Liz at this point would do them any good. Their businesses have done quite well, despite that early opposition from the Shandleys."

"Was Alan the one who made things tough for them?"

"No. Liz was the proverbial woman behind the man, in this case."

Something about the way she said that made Bea ask, "Buffy, how did you feel about those lawsuits?"

"Not one of their finer hours. But let's move on. Liz had other enemies, I fear. You can't serve on that many boards of directors and not have enemies!"

"Enemies who kill you?"

"It's implausible, I know." She hesitated a couple of seconds. "That Dr. Ramos is certainly a rude man, do you think he's unpleasant enough to commit murder?"

Well, Dr. R, there goes your endowment.

Bea decided to see what Buffy would say to something that was really bothering her. "Buffy, I honestly don't think anybody has a good enough motive to have killed Liz. But I'm worried about Javier."

Buffy's head jerked up and her eyes shot into Bea's. Her mouth was tight. "Really?"

"Well, I thought you knew... I mean I thought everybody knew that the tiles on those horrible mosaics match some of Maria's at their house. But I don't see how that means much; you know those one-color Mexican tiles are super common. And Maria's been gone for a couple of weeks, to Mexico, so she couldn't have cut the branch," Bea added quickly.

"Yes. Maria's gone. But Javier was devoted to Alan. I can't see Javier hurting Alan's widow. And as for those tiles... half of the people I know have them in their kitchens or patios or bathrooms!"

Bea almost mentioned that half of her acquaintances did *not* have custom hand-painted tile work, but what was the point of being rude? Instead, she replied, "I can't see any reason why Javier... or Maria... would hurt Liz. I completely agree with you."

"I'm glad to hear that, dear. I would hate for Javier and Maria to be scapegoats in this thing. I hope you can convince Detective Samuelson that you're right on this."

"Speaking of the tiles, do you usually leave that beautiful gate open? Is that how somebody left that datura mosaic in your courtyard?"

Buffy smiled. "That's a good question, my dear. I leave it open when I'm expecting someone. Like you, today. That time, I was expecting my gardener. It's easier than going out and unlocking it. And I never wanted one of those ugly automatic gates."

It's true they wouldn't fit with her décor. But it seems odd that a wealthy older woman living alone wouldn't take more precautions. But Bea kept this thought to herself. She didn't think she was going to get much more from Buffy. And if she stayed any longer, she might tell Buffy more than was wise.

"I really have to get home to my kids. My friend has been doing way too much childcare for me throughout this whole thing."

"Of course, Bea, I understand. Do take these cookies for your children. I don't need them."

"Well... thanks." Taking the cookies would give them both a graceful exit.

"Oh... and, Bea?"

Bea had gotten up to leave, but she paused. She sincerely hoped that Buffy was not coming up with some reason she had to stay and opine more about the murder.

"I don't have any grandchildren to give this to. Would your kids like it? It was mine as a child."

Buffy pulled a leather-bound volume off her bookshelf. Bea opened it carefully. The pages were yellowed and ripped, but the color plates were beautiful paintings of plants of the Eastern forests. Each had a children's rhyme beside it.

"This book got me started in loving plants. I know your kids won't be able to find most of these out here, but there are ferns and violets and wild strawberries up in the mountains." She turned to a plate near the middle, of a bunch of white violets. Beside it, in italic writing, was this verse: *Oh violet/, You're as sweet/ As any grander flower,/ And more complete.*"

"I always liked that poem as a little girl... I've always been small. Is your little girl built like you, Bea?"

"It looks that way."

"Well, take the book, then, and show her the violets."

"Thank you, Buffy."

On the way out, Bea caught a glimpse of the master bedroom. There was a lovely four-poster bed with a canopy and a matching chest of drawers, not mesquite, but cherry or walnut, more from her Eastern heritage, no doubt. On the chest of drawers there were six or eight bottles of medicine. The woman was obviously ill.

CHAPTER THIRTEEN

On the way back from Buffy's, Bea started thinking about Mount Lemmon, the 9,000-plus-foot peak that provided a mountain retreat to the desert dwellers in Tucson seven thousand feet below. It was a lot cooler up there. Cool sounded good. Bea was breaking out in prickly heat around her ankles and waist, something that happened when she was hot, humid, and stressed. And she had to admit; it wasn't just this damned investigation that was getting to her. The rash had appeared shortly after her last call to Frank. There were no messages from him on her cell, which confirmed her worst fears about his character.

There was plenty of weekend left. She and the kids could hop from their evaporative-cooled house to their air-conditioned car to other air-conditioned places like the library, or they could hang out in the cool pines. She pulled over and called up an old high school friend who'd already made it big and bought a cabin in Summerhaven, the town near the top of the mountain.

"Ann, is your Mount Lemmon cabin free tonight? I'd love to get my kids out of this heat."

"Yep, we're headed to Phoenix to see my folks. You know where the key is. Just one night?"

"Probably. They have a new camp on Monday, and I need to go to work."

"Any progress on that nasty murder case at Shandley?" Of course, Ann knew about it. Everybody knew. It needed to get solved so she could talk to people about something else.

"No breaks on the case. But I could sure use a night away. God, I would love to see some deep green up there. I've almost forgotten what it looks like. Do you think there's any water in Sabino Creek, or has it all dried up?"

"Maybe a little. Have fun!"

* * *

Bea picked her kids up from the Rices' and told them she had a surprise better than ice cream. They'd spend the night on the mountain and have s'mores. Jessie started jumping up and down at this, and Andy gave her a wide, beautiful smile.

Before they left Palo Verde Acres, Pat called and said he could take the kids on Sunday afternoon for a few hours.

"You're sure about this, Pat? Because we're headed up the mountain, and we don't want to come down before we have to."

"Yeah, there's a party I want to take them to, and there'll be a bunch of kids and a pool."

"Okay. Two o'clock? Back by suppertime? Six?"

"Fine."

Would that it was always so easy.

In about forty-five minutes, Bea had driven them along the winding highway right out of the lower desert and into the oak grasslands. They passed steep cliffs studded with saguaros. Her spirits rose with their heights and kept rising as she drove farther up the mountain. She pulled over at Molino Basin, on impulse, to have a "snack under the oaks." The trees provided welcome shade in the summer, despite the tiny, leathery leaves that kept them from losing too much water. But the cookie break didn't last long, because even at 4,400 feet the temperatures were not pleasant. "Come on, Mom, we need to keep going up!" Andy shouted.

Bea thought about a famous Mount Lemmon vegetation survey that showed that juniper trees had been common in Molino Basin in 1963. Now junipers could be found only 1,000 or more feet further up the mountain. It wasn't only humans that needed to climb to survive the effects of climate change.

They piled out in Ann's driveway high in the ponderosa pines, near the top of Mount Lemmon. Andy and Jessie had been to Ann's cabin several times and went straight to the games closet. This was the only place they could find *Candyland*. All those giant candy canes that Mom would buy only at Christmastime, but they could fantasize.

Bea threw together some spaghetti, which was always a hit. The kids saw it as a necessary prelude to s'mores. But they couldn't make a campfire; they were banned because of the wildfire danger. They'd have to roast marshmallows over the stove's gas burners. But at least there was an artificial fireplace they could sit around.

As they looked into the fake flames, Bea mused to herself that the southwestern United States was now essentially a perfectly laid fireplace, complete with dried out kindling and plenty of big wood ready to combust if any little spark escaped a cigarette, ATV, or marshmallow roasting. The pines around the cabin had burned five years ago. They, too, had been weakened by drought and beetles and they'd burned hot and quickly. Ann had bought the house at a very good price because so many people wanted out of the little community on top of the mountain, given both the charred landscape and the predictions of more of the same. There were expansive views now, but Bea missed the sense of enclosure, of privacy, that the thick woods had given her. The desert provided her wide views every day. The high mountain woodlands were about shelter from the sun, and sometimes shelter from all the world's realities, laid bare in the lowlands. She would have to find an unburned place on this mountain to experience that sense of seclusion she sought.

"Can we have thirds, Mommy?" Jessie asked.

"It's fourths," said Andy. Bea let them gorge themselves. They went to bed with visions of *Candyland*, high on enough sugar to need multiple bedtime stories. Bea had her own childhood memories of always-burnt hot dogs and marshmallows, roasted on countless campfires on this very mountain. Her parents hadn't had to rent a cabin to have a fire.

But she was here to throw all that off, the warming

planet, her children's environmental heritage, murder in her inner work circle, and traitorous men. Okay, so maybe Frank wasn't exactly traitorous, since he hadn't *told* her he wasn't involved with anybody else, but hadn't his behavior implied they were becoming intimate? And shouldn't he have at least mentioned a girlfriend? Or was Bea just out of touch with the dating world after almost eight years of marriage? Had Frank been offering simple friendship to a clearly over-whelmed single mom, and in her naïveté she'd thought he was implying more? After all, he'd told his mother that she was "a good friend."

One thing was clear. She was going to have to stiffen the part of her that had trusted Pat, and now Frank. She'd been a much-loved child, and Pat's betrayal had felt like the end of innocence. But clearly her innocence needed more scrubbing to wash out. She was too trusting about a possible murderer in her midst, too. Marcia was right, Bea *didn't* want it to be any of them; she still wanted it to be an outsider. She was just going to have to be more hard-headed about everything. Rub out the wishfulness. Find new resolve. She squared her shoulders.

But then she dropped her shoulders and rolled them around a few times. She exhaled a good long breath. All this self-talk about scrubbing and hardness and realism was not very relaxing. And what she most needed to do was relax.

She poured a glass of a very cold, very dry white wine and sat out on the porch looking at the Milky Way. A bat swooped by the roofline, and then two more came lower, directly into her field of vision. Faint sounds of a Mozart sonata blew like little gusts of wind from a neighboring cabin. A great-horned owl added some percussion. *Hoo-hoo, hoo, hoo.* The wind wafted the scent of the surviving ponderosa pines. Soothing but with a little sharpness to it, like Greek *ouzo.* The needles rustled with a warm breeze that blew a bit of hair into her eyes. She moved it slowly, and let the pine breeze seep into her tight shoulders, her tired eyes.

Her cell phone rang.

Bea almost didn't look to see who it was, but she did, and

it was Frank. She let it ring a few times. She decided to pick it up, but she'd hang up if he didn't apologize right away. She needed to see just how naïve she'd been.

"Bea, are you okay?"

"Yes, considering." There was a silence.

"I know I owe you an apology."

"I think so." But would he give her one?

He sighed. "You probably think I led you on and I suppose I did."

She didn't offer him the benefit of a response, so he continued, "Sherry and I were involved for a year before I moved out there. We didn't know if our relationship would weather the move. By the time I got back here, I knew things couldn't last with Sherry. And… more than that, I don't want them to. But we did have one last night together. Then we agreed to meet for lunch tomorrow for what we both know is our break-up conversation, and it will be over. Bea, Tucson feels like home to me, and Sherry has no interest in the 'horrible hot dry desert.'"

Bea started to say something, but he responded before she said it. "Yes, I get it that being involved with you… in any way… means being involved with three people. I need to take Andy and Jessie's feelings into account, as well." There was a silence. Then he continued, "I'd like to help you with whatever situation is going on right now, and I want to hang out with the three of you, wherever things take us. If that's okay with you."

I couldn't have asked for much more than that. Except that he hasn't actually broken it off with her yet, Bea told herself.

"Frank, it's really hard for me to trust you right now." *I just used that same phrase with Pat.*

"All you needed was another betrayal."

Well, he was a good listener.

"I don't want to think about betrayals and murders and humans' worst qualities right now, Frank. I'm up on Mount Lemmon looking at the Milky Way. Andy and Jessie are in bed, and I'm here with the bats and the owls and a glass of wine."

His voice was quiet. "I'm glad you're able to do that."

She almost said, "You would like it up here, Frank," but she didn't. She closed that gate in the fence between them.

"So, how are things in Virginia?" she asked, a little too brightly.

Frank hesitated a moment. "Bea, I've found out some really interesting stuff, and maybe more tomorrow. I don't want to bother you with it now. You don't need it, and I'm still not sure what the deal is. My plane gets back late tomorrow night. How about if I come by Monday morning, after the kids are on the bus? Seven forty-five, right?"

She nodded silently.

"Did you catch that?"

"Oh. Yes." *I don't know if I should have agreed so quickly. But this is business. This is my job, because I can't do the job I was hired for until this mess is cleared up.*

"So, we can take a walk in the desert by Shandley and I can tell you what I've discovered. Will Ethan mind if you're a couple of hours late for work?"

"I don't think so. I usually just work a half-day on Mondays; we're not open to the public."

"Great! So, Bea... please take care of yourself. You know what they say about how the parent should put on the oxygen mask before her kids. And in your case before the kids and all those people you work with."

"Thank you. I'm at nine thousand feet right now and there's more oxygen than I've breathed all week." *And you may have just increased the oxygen ratio. If you really follow through.*

Frank said, "I've heard that eighty percent of Americans can't see the Milky Way. My nephew saw it for the first time last year. God, I looked at it all summer every summer of my childhood. I'm glad Andy and Jessie aren't deprived of that yet."

"Where did you spend every summer of your childhood?"

"On a lake in New Hampshire. I think those summers are what led me to all the years working for the Forest Service and the Park Service. Bea, the oddest thing has happened this trip. I feel claustrophobic in the Virginia woods I grew up in. I can't see the horizon."

"I know exactly what you mean. Right at this moment, though, I'm enjoying the comfort of deep pine forest. Sometimes it's nice to hide out a bit."

This discussion was all very interesting, but Bea wanted to get back to being by herself in the night's quiet. "Frank, I need to go." She thought for a moment, and added, "Thank you for apologizing."

"Of course. I really am sorry about adding to your load."

"Also, thanks for not telling me about what you found out today. See you Monday."

"Until then, Bea."

She hung up and turned off her cell phone. She stared out at the stars. The Milky Way was even more distinct than it had been when she first came out on the porch. She focused on the Big Dipper. She knew it was part of a constellation called *Ursa Major.* The big bear. That's what she needed to be. Yes, she would defend her children like a mama bear, and she would retrieve the Bea that had knocked on the principal's door, more than twenty-five years before. But at that very moment, she would rather just take another deep breath of pine and let the wind blow her hair around.

She climbed under a blanket, for the first time in weeks, and fell asleep quickly. She was on a glass-bottomed sail-boat, blown by a gentle breeze. Marcia was on the boat with her, and they were trying to see some sea creature through the glass, but the water was so cloudy. The thing had lots of arms, sort of like an octopus, but the arms were human.

The sun came early and warm through the blinds. Jessie had climbed into bed with her at first light and was squirming around, trying to pull her mother out of bed. She wanted to go see the bear. Last time they had been up on the mountain they'd found bear tracks and scat near the cabin. Jessie had recently decided that she wanted to "work on bears" when she grew up. This expression came from hanging around some school friend's biologist dad, who "worked on butterflies." Bea was less than excited about the encounter between her child and a large mammal with formidable teeth and claws, but she thought it was good for Jessie to be able to identify bear sign. She made Jessie rehearse what she'd do if she saw a real bear... grab her mom's hand and tell her calmly where the animal was.

"Jessie, if we go to the creek, maybe we can find some of the flowers I want to see, and maybe a bear track for you?"

"What about for Andy?" Her kids were basically fair to each other, at least at this point. Adolescence was a long way off, thank God.

"Andy loves bugs. I'm pretty sure we can find some bugs."

The kids bolted their cereal so they could get out on the "hunt" right away. They started as far up the creek as they could, where there was a trickle of water and unburned beautiful Douglas firs and aspens. Bea found both yellow columbines and monkeyflowers. Andy stayed by a small rocky pool for an hour, simply watching the water striders and water boatmen. Bea and Jessie prowled around him, looking for bear tracks, and didn't find any, to Bea's relief.

A rock moved on the slope above them. "It's a bear with a white tail!" Jessie cried.

"It's a deer, honey," Bea said as it bounded off. Jessie stared up at the slope and broke into a smile.

"I didn't see it," her brother said. This made the find special to Jessie. But Andy had to get the last word in. "See, Jessie, you never know what'll happen. You look for something, and sometimes you find something completely different. But you always find *something*."

"Good advice, Andy." Bea just hoped that what she found wasn't a guilty friend.

"Ethan told me that when I was trying to find a roly-poly the other day. And Dr. Ramos said he was right. He said he'd found out stuff he never knew about Ethan!"

What was that about? "Time to head down the mountain!"

"Don't say it like it's a good thing, Mom," Andy said.

* * *

When they pulled up to the apartment complex, Pat was already there with his big SUV. Looking irked. Bea was five minutes late, and he didn't really have much call to be angry. After all, he'd completely reneged on his commitment from the day before. That's the way it always seemed to roll.

Jessie rushed for her dad and Bea admonished herself for feeling he didn't deserve it. If Jessie was happy, that was good. Andy was another story. He got into the back seat slowly and shot her a look as they drove off. It wasn't an unhappy look, exactly, but there was something about it that troubled her. On the mountain, he'd said that he wished they could stay up there all week.

So, she had Sunday afternoon off. She took a deep breath and forced herself to take a look at her messy little "unit." It was a definite step down from the last house she'd lived in with Pat. They'd had a back yard with a swing set, four bedrooms, a kitchen with plenty of counter space, and a front driveway suitable for bikes and trikes. She wasn't exactly pining for the old days; the physical comfort had not bound the emotional wounds. But now she had a wreck of another kind to deal with in this little house. Pieces of toys, lone socks in various bright colors, and mail and other no doubt important papers dotted the front rooms as if they'd somehow fallen from the ceiling. Her house wasn't raining meatballs, as one of her kids' books declared; it was raining essential bits of their lives.

She left the kids' room for them to clean, but she managed to make the rest of the place look as though it was *not* the scene of a criminal search. She bought the week's groceries, and was home a minute before six, Pat's supposed arrival time.

He was half an hour late, but he did bring back cheerful kids. "It was fun to see Josh again. How come we never see them anymore?" Andy asked.

"Maybe we can have Josh over soon," she said. That was doable. When this damned murder thing was over. This was turning into the flu that you thought would be short term, but that you were afraid might really change your life. The flu that might be something far worse than the flu.

"I'm starving, Mommy!" Jessie said. It was past their usual dinner time, which Pat no doubt knew. Fortunately, Bea had mini-pizzas in the freezer. They just had to choose their own toppings. Jessie insisted on blueberries for her one and only topping. Perfectly healthy, after all.

Andy read stories to his little sister after dinner. Bea exhaled and felt as though she'd been holding her breath for hours. She left the morning paper folded on the coffee table and picked up a light novel. She did check her email before bed.

There was nothing from Marcia, which she supposed was a good thing. Bea emailed her that she'd had a meeting with Buffy, hoping that Marcia wasn't working that late. Of course she was, and she wanted to talk to Bea first thing in morning.

"I need to meet with Frank early tomorrow. He just went to Virginia, and he may have some information about Davenport School, where Liz and Buffy went."

"Good. Okay, 10:00 then. At Shandley. I have other business there."

This would give Bea enough time to see what Frank had to say about a couple of things. She'd try to keep this meeting to his research about the murder, and she'd see if he brought up the break-up with Sherry.

She thought longingly of the cool breeze on the porch last night. She wished she could just go back up there instead of to Shandley, which was starting to feel like a cauldron of suspicious behavior. God, her whole life was turning into doubting other people.

A little rain would cool things off, too.

CHAPTER FOURTEEN

Frank was at the house at 7:45 a.m. sharp. He looked at her for permission, and they fell into an awkward short hug, the kind she'd give most any acquaintance. They took two cars to Saguaro National Park East, close to Shandley, and parked at the Tanque Verde Ridge Trail, which would lead them far into the Rincon Mountains if they'd had the time to hike seventeen miles up to Tanque Verde Peak. They walked up this billion-plus-year-old granite ridge side by side, crunching the dry vegetation by the side of the trail like corn chips. Frank asked her for the names of some of the plants... limberbush, dalea... but there wasn't much to marvel at. Pretty much everything had dried out, waiting for the rains for revival. The brittlebush had dropped its leaves. It was hard to remember how full and brilliantly yellow-flowered it had been just a couple of months ago. The ocotillos stood tall, having let go of their small leaves as soon as the weather dried out. Their long, barren, thorny stalks fanned out from the ground together. The prickly pear cactus pads were thin as cardboard, but there were big chunks eaten out of them by javelinas. The mammals had long since ceased activity. They'd be back at twilight.

Frank and Bea didn't say anything for a while. The cicadas were making so much noise that Bea wondered if they'd be able to talk. The gnats were coming out, too. Bea evolved a step/swat/step/swat routine. She watched a couple of lizards doing push-ups. It was still early enough for them to be active. Showing off for females, she'd heard. Was this what Frank was doing right now? Was he going to broach the subject of his relationship with Sherry? If not, he was a nice new acquaintance, and he was helping her solve this case. She could deal with that; she'd have to.

Frank finally began with, "So. Mom was a freshman when Liz and Buffy were seniors. They were glamorous, unattainable, soon to go beyond the cloister to college. But Mom has a friend who was in their class, and I had coffee with her."

Was he interested in this for a novel, or...

"And?"

"Buffy had a boyfriend named Alan. He was a dashing bomber pilot... you know the girls were in high school during World War II. She met him when she came out here to a dude ranch. She was over the moon for the guy."

"He must have been at the army air field that became Davis-Monthan Air Force Base here in Tucson. They trained bomber pilots. But wait a minute. Are you saying Liz stole Alan from Buffy?"

"Well, this first lady I talked to didn't know anything about that. She just remembered how head-over-heels Buffy was about the guy, and she thought they were still together at the Davenport graduation. But she sent me to another classmate who was closer to both Liz and Buffy. I talked to her on the phone right before I got on the airplane. She was chatty." He looked over at Bea before going on.

She obliged him. "So, what was she chatty about?"

"First of all, Bea, you have to realize that I didn't need to mention a murder investigation to this woman. She said it was already 'all over the Davenport grapevine.' And she's good at gathering gossip, as you will see."

Bea couldn't really blame Frank for a breach of confidence, considering that the murder was now public. This whole thing was expanding into every part of her life. Into the lives of people in Virginia and God knew where else, apparently. She was suddenly very impatient with Frank's carefulness. She was impatient with him, in general. Apparently, he hadn't broken up with Sherry. He would have told her by now, wouldn't he? "Spit it out, Frank."

He moved his head back in surprise, but then pulled himself back into alignment. He began quietly, "Okay. Well, first she told me about Liz at Davenport. Apparently, everybody envied her. According to her, Liz had 'looks, money, athletic prowess, social graces, and she was reasonably intelligent.' Note the order of her attributes."

Bea had to laugh.

"She also had a handsome, wealthy boyfriend from the University of Virginia—my alma mater, by the way. But it was only UVA, and for someone like Liz, having a boyfriend in an Ivy League college was far more prestigious."

"This sounds like a Jane Austen novel. Where are you going with this?"

"You'll see. Buffy went to Evans College, her mother's alma mater, which is in the San Francisco Bay area. Liz went to Blanchard, in Boston. Apparently, Alan had been at Harvard before he enlisted, and he went back after the war. So, he was a lot closer, geographically, to Liz, and they started dating. They fell for each other and got married. My chatty friend from Davenport knew that Buffy was devastated. Then the Davenport grapevine lost track of her. According to Mrs. Chatty: 'She was out there in the wilds of the West Coast, after all.' My mother's like that, too. The only *real* American civilization exists between greater Washington, D.C., and Boston.

"Anyway, Mrs. Chatty—okay, her name is Penelope Locks—did keep in touch with Alan and Liz and knew they moved to Tucson in the early fifties, a few years after Alan graduated from Harvard. Apparently, he preferred the 'wilds of the West Coast,' and had fallen in love with the Sonoran Desert when he was here during the war. He thought, correctly, it seems, that it was a great time to get into real estate in Tucson."

"Wow. So, when did Buffy and Greg Jones show up here?"

"Well, as I said, this Mrs. Locks lady didn't keep in touch with Buffy. But she did hear, 'through the grapevine,' that Buffy had married well and happily, and that she and her husband moved to Tucson a few years after the Shandleys. She'd also been told that Buffy and Liz had rekindled their old friendship. They'd come to a Davenport reunion and

Mrs. Locks was sniffing around for tension between them. Liz told her she was being ridiculous. She played field hockey with Buffy in an old blue-team, red-team rematch, and they were dynamite together. 'So, I believe the rift was healed… as far as anyone can know these things, young man,' she said to me."

Bea had to admit that Frank was a good detective. *I can live with him as just a friend. I was being absurd to think there was anything else happening between us. The most important thing is to solve this murder, and he's helping with that.*

"Okay… so, what do you make of all this?"

"Well, on the face of it, Buffy certainly could have a motive for murdering Liz. Jealousy. But my God, Bea, it's several decades too late! It doesn't make any sense to me."

"I agree with you. It's unlikely. I don't know if it's more likely that Myron killed her for his inheritance, or that Dr. Ramos killed her to remake the board and have her bequest fund his career plans. Those issues are at least relevant *now*. I guess Ethan could have killed her because she knew something about his past felony, or even that he was hoping for an endowment for Shandley? Javier could have killed her because she always treated him badly, and she was unfaithful to the spirit of her husband. And Maria could have helped him. But I don't think so. Or, like the newspaper implied, for that matter, it's as likely that Alicia—or Raoul—killed her for blocking the Vargases' career rise. *That* was a long time ago, too."

"It's a good thing you're off the hook. You might have wanted to kill her for blocking your climate change class series."

"I was thinking that myself, the other day. Frank, I just have such a hard time seeing what could possibly have motivated anyone to go that far. And then there are some physical difficulties. I don't see how Alicia called her and pulled the branch down when she was with Angus. I don't see how Buffy could climb up in that tree and saw that branch. And then climb down and pull it down on her. Myron's not too spry, either. But it's the motive thing that makes the least sense."

They'd been walking steadily up the slope, and it was already ninety degrees. They were sweating, and Bea was glad she didn't need to impress anyone when she went to work. Which she needed to do soon. They stood for a moment at an overlook, and watched the cars scuttling across the flat street grid of the Tucson Valley below.

"Beetle races," said Frank.

"Exactly."

Bea suggested that they take a little break in a dry wash that crossed the trail. They went up it a bit and found a place where the high rocks provided a bit of shade. They weren't going to find shade from trees; the mesquites and palo verdes weren't big enough for that.

"Frank, I don't like it that the mosaic pieces match the ones at Javier's house, the ones that Maria uses. If they didn't do the awful deed, it kind of feels like somebody is trying to frame them."

"Who doesn't like them?"

"Myron, apparently. Angus said Alan Shandley wanted him to be more like Javier. A manly outdoorsman."

"Okay, who else?"

"Not Buffy. She's really upset that he's implicated. I don't see why Ethan would have anything against him. Or Alicia, who's sort of off the hook, except, as you pointed out, the media *is* hot on the story of her old feud with the Shandleys."

"Did you read yesterday's paper?"

"No, when I got down from the mountain, I couldn't bear to. I read a novel instead. The paper's still folded on my kitchen counter. Why?"

"There's a story you might want to read. About the Vargases. But go ahead and tell me the rest of what you've been thinking."

I'm wondering if you broke up with Sherry, or if you're even going to mention anything about it, damn it. She didn't say it though.

"Well, Dr. Ramos seems to respect Javier. Heck, I don't know. Maybe he thinks that with Javier out of the way, he's more likely to get hired at Shandley. Angus found out that Dr. R is probably not going to get tenure, so he's angling for a position. I kind of doubt he'd like Javier's wages, though."

"I'm sure you're right on that score. I did do a little more research on Javier's family history on the land that Shandley is part of."

When she looked surprised, he said, "I did that before I left Tucson. The university library has great resources. You told me that Marcia said Javier's family once owned the property."

"Yes, I guess I did."

"So, Mexican ranchers often sold out to the big Anglo cattlemen, but that wasn't always just for economic reasons."

"Marcia implied something like that, too. Did you find some story about Javier's ancestors?"

"Yep. Javier's forefathers believed an Anglo rancher who said he'd pay the taxes on their land in return for some work they did for him. Then the rancher claimed the land was *his* since he was the taxpayer. Of course a judge agreed with him."

"What a cheat."

"So, it does seem that Javier, like Buffy, and like Alicia, has a legitimate old grievance. But Javier's beef isn't against the Shandleys per se, and I don't see why he would act on it now. So, there we are. Or rather, there we aren't. Round and round it all goes."

"But I keep wondering about all the references to environmental issues. The roses and the tulips. The rose between Liz's teeth in that mosaic 'art' thing, and I think there was a rose pin on her shirt, too. And somebody dropped a tulip pin near the murder site. And Armando Ramos and Angus, of course, really want to get rid of the big rose and tulip gardens. And then... I'm not sure if I told you about this, but there was a page of a scientific paper about climate change near the murder site. Could Dr. Ramos have dropped it there? Could he be trying to make a point about climate change with all this roses and tulips stuff? I mean, is he just unbalanced enough to salt the Gardens with roses and tulips to show his disapproval?"

"You know him better than I do. I'm sure I don't know. It seems awfully bizarre, though."

They headed down the hill and Bea stumbled over a root. "I'm the one who's unbalanced. In more ways than one."

"I'll do what I can to help you stay upright, Bea."

She looked at him. It seemed sincere.

"You haven't asked me about Sherry," he said.

"That's for you to tell, on your own. You've been a 'good friend' about helping with the murder stuff. I appreciate that. Anything else between us is separate." She felt she'd said this in a professional way.

"I guess I was waiting for you to ask. I figured that when you didn't ask, you'd moved beyond it being important to you, and that would be entirely fair. Sorry, again. You were waiting for *me* to tell. Damn it." He stopped talking and turned to look at her. "It's over, Bea."

Her mind heard that it was over between her and Frank, but his expression said otherwise.

"I talked to Sherry. Logistically, we can't manage a relationship where neither one of us wants to be where the other one is. But the logistics point to a much bigger problem. She's way less experimental than I am. She likes the corridors of power in D.C.; she cares about status and money far more than I do. The track I'm on—becoming an indigent writer and desert rat—is completely unappealing to her. The inverse is true for me. I'm open now, Bea. But I understand if you don't feel comfortable with any kind of intimate relationship. I really do."

Open. That was an interesting word. She realized that during this whole walk, she'd been hunching her shoulders together. She turned to face him and pulled her shoulders back. She looked at him for a moment and he held her gaze. Then she walked up to him and hugged him. They held on a little longer than they did earlier that morning.

At a certain point, I have to trust someone, right?

They were quiet as they walked to the parking lot. There was a bit of awkwardness as they parted. Bea looked him in the eye and said, "Thanks, Frank. A lot." And she touched his arm, sliding her fingers down it quickly, before she got into the car. His arm felt good and solid and muscular and she realized she wanted him to hold her. She wanted to be able to lean on somebody else instead of always being the one who had to be strong.

But she wasn't ready for that. She turned the car key. "I have to go to work. But thanks again. For everything." She looked at him and wondered if he knew what *everything* was.

A different live news truck was at Shandley when she pulled in. She'd better jerk herself out of romantic fantasies. Quickly.

CHAPTER FIFTEEN

An earnest-looking well-moussed male reporter was shoving a microphone at Alicia in the Shandley Gardens parking lot. Alicia had already half-turned away from him. "I have no comment," she said, and headed for the doors. The reporter and cameraman tried to follow her, but Angus appeared from the side of the building and blocked the front door. He motioned Bea in, because they were already after her, asking if she had any comment about the latest revelations.

"I have no idea what you're talking about," Bea demurred, and made a quick dash for her office, locking the door. Again. *So much for the positive things in life.* Time to focus. She called Angus on his cell.

"You're in kind of late, Bea. You missed the action."

"Now what?"

"The media found out about Ethan's drug conviction. That's what they were asking Alicia about. She wasn't on the board when he was hired. She stalled them but who knows what will happen now. Also, they dug up from somewhere that Ethan is about to have a personnel evaluation. He told somebody at the gym, a couple of weeks ago, that Liz Shandley didn't 'think he was up to snuff for her garden.' That she was looking for an excuse to hire somebody more prestigious. God knows how the news media finds these people. It was stupid of Ethan to trust this gym guy, though. Although Ethan probably didn't think what he was complaining about was newsworthy at the time."

"Maybe the gym guy works out with Armando. He said something mysterious about finding out something about

Ethan. He said it to Andy."

"Wonderful. Remind me never to talk to Armando about anything ever. But there's something else. An article in yesterday's paper about the Vargases."

"I just heard about that. I guess I'd better read it."

"Yep, you'd better. I'm sure it's online."

She exhaled. "Well, this should last another few news cycles. Can we just close Shandley until Marcia gets this figured out and go on unpaid leave? Swimming in the ocean sounds nice."

"I like that idea. Although I doubt your friend Marcia would like it. Anyway, I think we all need you here to make sure she's on the right track."

"If I'm lucky I'll get in a swim in a pool. That's about as close to the ocean as I'm likely to get."

When she hung up, she thought about talking to Ethan. She wasn't sure what she'd say, but she opened her door and walked to his office. The door was closed, and she wasn't about to intrude by knocking. She might as well read the damned article about the Vargases. And give up on Gardens work. She'd already determined her job now was solving the murder, and at this point, why would Ethan say otherwise?

She found the Vargas article in the online edition of the *Post*. The reporter had dug up the Cactus Club controversy, including Raoul Vargas's description of Alan as a "bigot." But there was more. The enterprising reporter had also found some uncle of Raoul's who'd said that the family was glad both Liz and Alan were gone now. "They were the kind of Tucsonans that held us all back. My nephew is too polite to say this, but it's the truth." Raoul Vargas was quoted as saying that his uncle's views did not represent his, or those of his wife, who had chosen to be on the board of Shandley Gardens because she so appreciated this contribution of Alan's to Tucson. Alicia was quoted, too: "I deeply regret Mrs. Shandley's death, and the violence that caused it. Violence is never the solution to disputes, real *or* imagined. In this case, the *Tucson Post* is fabricating a current dispute between our families. This old dispute is long since over."

Bea thought this whole thing looked like a way for the reporter to make a name for himself, and not much more. But maybe she was wrong. *That* was certainly possible.

Marcia called just as she finished the article and said she'd be half an hour late for their 10:00 meeting. Bea decided to find somebody to interview.

Javier was weeding outside her window. She went out into the heat and asked, "Hey, Javier. Do *you* have any brilliant new insights into this murder?"

"Nope. I was hoping you were close to figuring it out."

"Not yet. Javier, you don't say much, but you see a lot. Is there anything you've thought about that could be helpful? You knew Alan and Liz for decades. How could she have made someone hate her enough to kill her?"

"You know I don't like this kind of talk. But I'll tell you what I know, because maybe it will help you find the real murderer. Bea, Liz was a lonely woman. She knew lots of people, but I never felt they were real friends, you know? Maybe Buffy, I don't know. Liz pushed people away. Even Alan. I hated it when she talked about what *he* wanted, after he died. Like about how he would've wanted to keep the lawn. She didn't really know that part of him. When he retired, he wanted to spend all of his time in the garden partly to keep out of all those parties and meetings she wanted him to go to. He would say, "Another night, another fundraiser." He told me he wished he'd been a farmer. I don't believe that; he liked expensive wine and cigars and trips to Costa Rica too much." Javier raised his eyebrows in dismissal. "I would have liked his money, but I would not have traded my life for his."

"It was an unhappy marriage?"

"Who can really know? *Quién sabe?* But yes, I think so."

"And how did Myron figure in?"

"That was one thing I didn't respect Alan for. He pushed Myron too hard when he was little. Of course, I didn't know any of them then, but Alan told me about taking Myron hunting and backpacking, and the kid hated all of it. Alan wanted his son to be like him. You know, a good businessman, a jungle explorer, *muy macho*, you know? But Myron didn't want any of that stuff."

"Did Liz protect him from Alan's pushing? Maybe he was resentful of her as well as Alan for all that."

"I don't know. Myron was in his twenties by the time I met him. He shared a lot of things with his mom by then. He liked being part of Tucson's rich. It seemed like they got closer as he got older, more involved with the business and on more boards and things like that. He started going to those fundraisers with her and Alan was happy about that, because then he didn't have to go."

"Was Myron always single?"

"Bea, I know that Alan was afraid his son was gay. He even said that to me, once, and I said, 'So what if he is?' Alan never mentioned it again." Javier gave a snorty kind of laugh. Bea raised an eyebrow, and he continued, "But I don't know. Myron was with a woman, an artist, for a lot of years. I don't think his parents ever thought she was good enough for him, but that doesn't stop most people who are in love. Still, she moved to New York, and I heard she told him to come or else, and he didn't go. Who knows the real reason why? But I think Myron will be better off now, he'll feel he can do what he wants, finally. He's free of all those expectations."

"Well, Javier, isn't that a pretty good motive to kill Liz?"

"I don't know. Lots of things I don't know. Myron does things I don't understand. But I can't picture him doing something that... *aggressive.* But maybe. *Tal vez.* Who really sees inside another person?"

Who indeed? I don't have such a good track record, she thought. What she said was, "And Buffy? Does she care as much about Liz as she seems to?"

"I don't know. I keep saying that. How can I tell you what's between two women like that? They're different from me. But Buffy has been kind to me and to Maria. Kinder than Mrs. Shandley. Always generous at Christmas and when our children were born. She helped two of our kids with college tuition. She and Mr. Jones came to our kids' graduations. She had no kids of her own, so she took on others—Myron, a long time ago. And she was kind of an aunt to ours. She told me to call her Buffy. Liz never said, 'Just call me Liz.'" They both laughed at that idea.

Bea kept up her questions. "You worked for Buffy, right?"

"Yes, Maria and I both did. Maria sometimes cooked for her, and they made green corn tamales together from scratch once a year."

"So you don't think Buffy killed Liz."

"I don't *feel* it was her."

"Like I don't *feel* it's you or Maria. Okay. Another question, since I'm now playing amateur detective so that the wrong person doesn't get nabbed and the right one does. You've known Alicia for a while, too, right?"

"Not really. But we have some distant relatives in common. But I can tell you one thing."

"Shoot."

"That story about the Cactus Club? Alan hated all that. Liz made him do it. He regretted that lawsuit and he apologized to me about it and to Alicia and her husband Raoul. Alan told me that. I think Alicia respected him, in the end. I think that's one reason she agreed to be on the board."

"So how did she feel about Liz?"

"How would you feel about Liz if she got lawyers to keep you out of the place where business deals happen, saying you shouldn't be there because you have brown skin? It could sure hurt your business. Would you kill somebody for that? Maybe some people would. But it's not like it wrecked Alicia's life. She's happy now… at least I think she is."

He sounded uncertain for a moment, and Bea looked up at him. "Do you doubt that?"

"It's nothing. She seemed a little sad the other day, but it could be anything. It could be these reporters opening up old wounds that were almost healed."

"Probably." But Bea wondered. "Okay, Javier, what about Armando Ramos? You get along with him, right? How do you *feel* about him as the murderer?"

"He's a good botanist. He respects my work and I respect his. But we're not friends. He hated Liz's views on his research, and he sort of wants to remake the Gardens in his own image."

"Do you think he could have done it? Killed Liz?"

"Bea, I do not know him, not really, I can't get inside his mind." Javier was fundamentally not a gossip, although she was pushing him to be, as hard as she dared.

"I know you need to take care of the plants and not just my curiosity. But I said I don't *feel* it's you or Maria. Can you help me out here? Help me find some good reasons why I don't *think* it could be you or Maria?"

"Maria was in Mexico. She couldn't have done anything but make those mosaics. And all you have to do is look at her tile style. Those are crude. There's messy grout every-where. Maria's work is careful, artistic. And never of people. Flowers, animals, yes. She does not make fun of people. I told the detectives all of this. They already looked at her work. They can check out her character. No one will say she makes fun of people. No one will say she's a messy artist. She's the kind of person who dusts our house twice a week."

"How do we get you two off the hook?"

"I mean, I could have done all that with the saw and everything, I'm strong enough. But is it in *my* character? I told the detectives to talk to my priest, my neighbors, and the people at Big Brothers. I work with gang kids, you know. I hope your friend will talk to those people."

"Good, I'm glad you've talked to Marcia about all that. She only gives me bits and pieces of what's going on."

"Oh, I told her, all right. Bea, may I ask you a favor?"

"Sure."

"Maria has come back. She didn't want me to go through this by myself. Could you just go by and maybe make her feel a little better? Just on your way home. You know where we live. It's out of the way, I know, but maybe a short visit?"

"Sure," she said again.

"I have to get back to work. Thanks, Bea. *I* feel a little bet-ter."

"I wish I did."

When Bea headed back to her office, she noticed that the boardroom was starting to fill up. *What now?* She didn't have much time to think about it, because Marcia came in just then, and shut Bea's door behind her.

Bea sat at her desk, but Marcia remained standing. Bea gave Marcia as much detail as she could about the visit with Buffy and about Frank's research. She also went through the whole memorial service, but it turned out that the police had sent someone there, so Marcia had a good handle on that event.

"Your takeaways from all this?" Marcia finally asked.

"My mind's a stew that needs more time to simmer."

"Good. Let me know if you think the stew's ready for tasting." Marcia cracked a smile.

Bea gave her old friend a serious look. "How close are you to knowing, Marcia?"

"Getting there." Javier wasn't the only one who was being tight-lipped.

Marcia opened the door and said she was headed out to the eucalyptus grove again. So Bea walked out into the hall to see what was up. The board room door was still closed and so was Ethan's door. Bea walked by quietly. She could hear him on the phone in his office, talking in a low, urgent tone. She was *not* going to stand there and eavesdrop.

She returned to her office and started to make some notes for herself about who could be the guilty party. But then Ethan knocked on the door. She wondered what his agenda was, but he just sank into the chair in front of her desk and was quiet. He ran his hand through his hair. It looked like this wasn't the first time he'd done that today. There was a spot of something that looked like egg yolk on the front of his shirt. Should she mention it to him? He'd had an extra shirt around when he'd needed one before, the day of the murder. But he spoke first.

"There's something I'd like to say to you, Bea. Your kids add a lot to the Gardens."

She expected something about the patio garden tour, or the murder investigation. This was curious.

Ethan continued, "I don't have any siblings, so I don't have any nieces and nephews, much less kids of my own. My family's not close. But I like providing an environment here where kids are welcome. As long as it doesn't interfere with work, of course." Then he looked her straight in the eyes and said, "I kind of look at the Gardens as a tribe, albeit a young one, all focused around this piece of land. I hope we can continue on this way, after all this craziness is over. The media mess will die down eventually. We're good underneath it all."

Bea hoped he wasn't giving his goodbye address. Life had gone completely bizarre; her boss was talking about how much her kids added to the Gardens, while she typed out a story for the police about two board members' entwined history, which may have resulted in the death of one of them.

From the boardroom, there were sounds of chairs scraping the floor and voices raised in goodbyes. Ethan returned to his office, leaving Bea's door ajar. Bea watched the board members' exit. Alicia strode out first, with her jaw set. Myron came next, and he was paler than ever, if that were possible. The black bags under his eyes had turned bluish. He was walking with Buffy, who looked like a little tropical bird in her flowered linen dress. Dr. Ramos trailed them all, with a creeping ironic smirk. He was at war with his mouth, trying to keep it from tipping up at the corners. He was the only one who spoke to her, through the half-open door. "The drama mounts."

"What happened?" She didn't know if she was supposed to ask, but she wasn't going to hold back now.

Alicia seemed to have heard their exchange and she came back, giving Dr. Ramos a warning look. "Bea, the staff will hear what we talked about shortly. I'll be putting out a press release."

Ethan's door was closed. *Was he fired?*

Bea's half-day was up, and she needed to get the kids. Then she'd honor her promise to visit Maria. She parked the car in the camp parking lot and checked her email on her cell phone. The press release was there.

The board affirmed that they knew that Ethan had had a troubled past, but that he had made a complete turn-around in his life. They believed in the importance of second chances and said that Ethan had excelled in college and graduate school, as a nurseryman, *and* as Shandley's Executive Director. Mrs. Vargas, as President of the Board of Directors, also wanted to state her respect and affection for both Alan and Liz Shandley and her deep sorrow and concern over Mrs. Shandley's untimely death.

At least Alicia was acting like a reasonable adult in all this. She wasn't giving the media much grist for the gossip mill.

Bea called Angus. She needed somebody else's take on these latest developments.

"Yeah, I read the release, all right," he said. "Myron knew about the conviction, because he and Liz and Buffy hired Ethan. But I'm thinking Alicia didn't know and was blindsided by this," Angus said.

"Well, Liz and those guys probably should have told the others on the board about their decision to hire a convicted felon. I think it's fine. I think Ethan's a good director, too, but it wasn't fair to the others to keep them in the dark." She took a breath. "So, Angus, where does this leave us?"

"I have no clue. But here's something else. Okay, I've turned into a despicable spying sort of person. You must admit this situation brings it out in all of us. Anyway, I saw Buffy and Myron talking on a garden bench before they went into the meeting. Myron was so animated that he caught my attention. He had his hand on Buffy's shoulder and was talking a mile a minute. I couldn't hear anything they said. Then he asked her something and she burst out crying. They fell into each other's arms, and I didn't really want to keep watching. It was so intimate."

"Angus, this whole thing is starting to feel like a whole lot of us are being kept in the dark about a whole lot of things."

"Truer words were never spoken."

CHAPTER SIXTEEN

Andy and Jessie were delighted about visiting Tia Maria. She always had some treat in her house or her handbag or her pocket even. When they showed up at the modest frame house in South Tucson, Jessie's eyes went right to the kitchen cabinet that housed sugary delights. Maria laughed and looked at Bea for permission. She nodded, and Maria produced a jar full of *leche quemada.* The kids loved the simple sugary candy with the vanilla flavor.

"Two only," Bea said.

Maria offered her coffee, which Bea turned down.

"That might get in the way of any sleep I'll be lucky enough to get." She hadn't had any lunch, but she was too wired up to be hungry. She did accept Maria's offer of *jamaica,* a delicious deep-red beverage made from hibiscus flowers.

"Maria, I have no idea how you've managed to create candies and iced tea in the brief time you've been back from Mexico."

"It's easier than trying to figure out the murder. *Pobrecita.* But it's good for us that this detective trusts you."

"All I can say, Maria, is that I am doing my best to figure it out. Is there anything you can tell me that will help you and Javier?" Maria looked over at the kids playing fetch with a little white dog, and Bea's eyes followed hers.

Maria called to them, "Can you kids take this darned dog out of here? He needs to run around outside! It's not so hot under the mesquites in the back yard."

"Okay, Tia Maria," Andy said, and they vanished out the kitchen door.

"Bea, you can look at my work on the side patio. It doesn't

look much like the pictures Javier told me about, those mosaic pictures of Liz."

"Okay, I'll do that. But anything else?"

"Well, I don't like to say things about people I don't really know. But my husband takes that too far. He saw Myron Shandley looking over the fence at my patio a few nights ago. You know Myron doesn't come around this neighborhood. I don't think he was just walking by."

"No. Probably not. I'd love to see your work, Maria."

Maria led her out. They went from the bright yellow kitchen with red, blue, and white-striped curtains to the living room, which was equally bright with chair and couch cushions embroidered with geometric and animal designs. The walls were full of family photographs—babies, athletic teams, graduations, weddings, Christmases. A real contrast with Buffy's dour ancestral portraits, Bea thought.

The patio, too, was full of color. This was where Javier tended his cactus and succulent specimens. They weren't in flower in late June, but their containers made up for their lack of blooms.

"Your work?" Bea asked.

"Yes," Maria said. The planters had intricate tile pictures of plants and their pollinators—long agave flower stalks, their greenish-yellow flowers visited by long-nosed bats; red tubular penstemon flowers pollinated by brilliant hummingbirds; daisy-like desert marigolds surrounded by bees. There were concrete benches there, too, with desert scenes—a pack of javelinas framed by the saguaros in the Rincon Mountain foothills, a mother Gambel's Quail, surrounded by her brood, crossing an arroyo amid orange poppies and purple lupines. The work was beautiful by anyone's standards.

"I have a new contract, with Branson's," Maria said. Branson's was the most expensive nursery in Tucson.

"You surely deserve it, Maria." How could anyone think Maria was the creator of the awful Liz pieces? Those horrible mosaics were crudely put together, using the biggest tiles possible and messy, messy grout. There was no artistry to them, and no one could be uplifted by viewing them. Maria's pieces, on the other hand, were intricately put together, using all the colors of the spectrum. They were a tribute to the beauty of the desert.

"Thank you for your hospitality and for showing me your work," Bea said. "I'll point out the difference between it and those awful portraits of Liz. I'll bet the police have already noticed, though. And I'll mention that Myron was hanging over your fence."

"*Muchas gracias, amiga.*"

Bea tried to have a normal evening with the kids and was marginally successful, at first. But at dinner, Andy pulled his ear and asked, "Have you figured out why Mrs. Shandley died, Mom?" She was glad he didn't use the word *murder* again.

"No, honey. We're working on it." Andy nodded, but he crawled off into a corner with his books for the rest of the night.

"Don't worry, sweetie, we'll get it figured out," she said, as she smoothed his hair at bedtime. Yet another incentive—and maybe the most important one of all—to get this damned case wrapped up.

With the kids asleep, Bea was checking her work email before bed that night (a bad habit she needed to curb). There was a message from Myron. He wanted to take her to lunch. This was another first. She wasn't naïve enough this time around to see it for anything other than what it was. He wanted to know what Marcia thought.

Oh, well, it couldn't hurt. Maybe he'd say something that would give him away as a matricidal maniac. But Myron acted too constrained to be a maniac. He'd always seemed a little like a dog on a leash with two masters, Liz and Buffy. He'd appeared to be unleashed and actually happy for a bit, right after Liz's death, but as this investigation dragged on, he was more tense than ever. He had to know that he was a prime suspect. Bea was certainly anxious about the goings-on, too, but it would be so much worse if she might be accused of murder.

As she drifted off to sleep, Bea thought she heard raindrops. She made herself wake up to celebrate, but it was only a cat on the roof. She dreamed of rain moistening the desert, bringing out the sharp scent of the creosote, greening everything.

* * *

In the morning, the radio said the afternoon high could reach a "record-breaking 112 degrees." And there was a 30% chance of late afternoon showers.

She called Marcia from the office and told her she'd be dining at the Cactus Club with Myron at noon. She didn't dare walk the grounds all morning, because they were swarming with gossipy locals. Maybe the afternoon highs would clear them out. She was supposed to *want* visitors to Shandley; this was all wrong.

The retired English professor volunteer was back collecting admissions. "No time to reread Tolstoy today. You're making me work for a living again!" he said. "But really, Bea, did we need to resort to murder to up the visitation?"

"I agree there must be a better way."

"Let's just stage *Macbeth* in the rose garden instead. It'd be far less stressful."

Ethan had put a note on his office door saying he was feeling "under the weather" and would work from home.

Bea decided that Angus might know something about the Vargases. He'd been at Shandley when Alicia came on the board.

She found Angus working on another clogged irrigation emitter. The last time she'd found him doing this the world had been a relatively benign place.

"Angus, why did Alicia come on the board if Liz and Alan had been so awful to her in the past? I could see forgiving them, but isn't it quite an act of forgiveness to actually come on the board of the garden created by somebody who'd try to keep you down, both professionally and socially?"

"I've been thinking about that, Bea. I'm pretty sure Liz didn't recruit Alicia. I think Buffy did. But why did Alicia accept? Do you suppose she was planning some sort of revenge by sabotaging the place? As far as I can see, she's a much more effective board president than Liz was."

"I don't know. Maybe she really is just a responsible community member who is forgiving and loves public gardens. Or maybe there's something there that I don't get."

"I just hope Javier doesn't get nailed."

"Me, too. Angus, I've got to go. I'm having lunch with Myron. At the Cactus Club."

Angus was speechless at this.

Bea was again hit with the odd position she was in. Myron, like Buffy, was her boss's boss. Yet he was inviting her to lunch, and her boss was under suspicion... at least she thought he was. And she was trying to assess this board member's guilt in a murder investigation.

* * *

The Cactus Club was in an old adobe building that belied the prices on its menu. It had been an Anglo businessman's venue for many decades; they'd finally allowed women into the club only after they'd allowed non-whites in the door. There was an inner courtyard, with the requisite shade umbrellas and misting machine. The Club was famous for its murals, she knew, depicting scenes of Tucson's history.

She and Myron were escorted to what the waiter knowingly called his "usual table," in front of a whole wall painted with priests tending gardens and orchards under "A" Mountain, which had been Tucson's birthplace, owing to its then-permanent water source. There was a Tohono O'odham village painted on another wall. The Tohono O'odham, or Desert People, had lived in the Tucson area before the arrival of the Spanish, and they were an important part of Tucson's current cultural mix. Bea thought there was a certain irony that many of the people the mural highlighted wouldn't have been allowed inside the club until quite recently, except as paintings on a wall. The third mural showed Tucson as the territorial capital in the 1860s, with horses clopping by one-story adobe buildings. All the people depicted were Anglos in Victorian dress, uniquely ill-suited to the desert climate.

She hoped the Cactus Club's food was as good as the art-work, but that was not to be.

The club had evolved somewhat beyond its steakhouse origins in that it had a few meat-heavy salads, but Bea was glad she wouldn't have to spend her own $18 on one. She ordered a Cobb salad and iced tea and settled into her chair to see what Myron had in mind. Just as he seemed about to ask an important question—he picked up a fork in a ques-tioning sort of gesture—a couple of businessmen of his age came by and asked, "Who's this charming young lady, Myron?"

Before Bea could register her full horror at being taken for Myron's girlfriend, he stopped them short. "Bea works at Shandley, gentlemen. This is a business lunch."

"Quite a lot of goings-on there lately. Hope they catch Liz's killer soon. We'll leave you to it."

The men walked off, but Bea caught a glance between them that implied they didn't believe Myron. Men's clubs apparently still encouraged this kind of behavior, even if they had let women in. Bea's mother had attended a service club meeting when the members gave the club president—a woman—a sexy teddy as a birthday present. And that had been in the late nineties.

She and Myron started off talking about the Fourth of July, of course. They *were* seated under "A" Mountain after all. Yes, she told Myron, she wouldn't miss seeing if "A" Mountain caught on fire this year since the fire trucks were always ready. And yes, she did have two kids. Did he have any chil-dren? (That could provide a new twist, if there was another heir nobody knew about). But Myron didn't admit to any descendants. Finally, after they'd both had too many chips and plenty of salsa, Myron asked her if "her friend Detective Samuelson" had any leads. He said he could hardly bear the stress of losing his mother *and* wondering about the motives of everyone around him.

She told Myron what she'd told Buffy. That Marcia asked her questions, but didn't tell her much.

"But surely you have some idea of her current thinking?"

"Not really."

He'd have to show his cards. He twisted his ring on his right hand. It was a nice Hopi silver overlay band with a prominent turquoise, and it was loose, as if he'd lost weight recently.

"I understand that the awful mosaics match some tiles at Javier and Maria's house."

How did he know that? She didn't think Marcia had told him. But who knew what leaked and how? *This* better not get to the press. Ungrateful lifelong employee is prime suspect.

She played dumb. "I'm really not privy to all the police discussions and disclosures, Myron. Sorry."

"Bea, I heard Javier telling Angus about it. I guess I'm just concerned that my mother's killer is still on the loose. I don't think Javier liked Mom much. She didn't care about the garden the way he and Dad did."

Bea chose not to do him the favor of reacting. She crunched some iceberg lettuce and desiccated chicken breast and looked up. "That's too bad, Myron."

Myron affected nonchalance, too, as he made his next announcement. "You know my mother tried like hell to keep this an *Anglos-only* club." Bea shook her head as if to say she didn't know. What it really meant was "No, I don't know what your take is on this story. Tell me."

He continued. "The Vargases brought a lawsuit against this place when I was still at the University of Arizona. They felt, as members of Tucson's business community, that they should be able to dine with the rest here. I remember hearing Mom say they had to stop this, because everything worked better when 'Mexicans stayed in South Tucson.' Dad didn't really want to fight this battle, but he did, to keep the peace. Of course they lost."

"Yes, fortunately. But why are you telling me this?"

"Oh, I don't know. When Mother said something about how the Gardens couldn't really afford to give Javier a raise, because Ethan announced he was doing that, Alicia said something snide like, 'You never did believe in equality, did you?' It was kind of under her breath, between the two of them. But I heard it."

"Wow." *I guess people feel free to test their theories on me, in a way they wouldn't with Marcia. Maybe that's good. Maybe this will all lead somewhere.*

They both indulged in platitudes about how they hoped this would wrap up soon, and how it was wearing on everyone, but that Shandley's reputation would survive. It was just too good not to. Over dessert (Myron insisted she have some, and there was a nice-sounding peach champagne sorbet on the menu), he brought up the people he hoped would *not* be accused.

"Speaking of people suffering, Buffy's going through a lot right now. Surely she's not in Detective Samuelson's sights."

"I don't know." This was true. She wished she knew as much about the investigation as everyone at Shandley seemed to think she did.

Myron gave her a long look before he said the inevitable. "I do realize that the one who gets an inheritance is always suspect. But you know how devoted I have always been to my mother. Surely nobody can seriously suspect me of murdering my own mother!"

"Myron, it doesn't seem likely you'd do that, but as I said, Marcia just asks me stuff. She keeps her suspicions to herself. I'm sorry, I really can't help you. I know it has to be agonizing. Sorry." And she was sorry. She didn't like to see people in agony, even if they weren't her favorite people.

It was a generally unsatisfactory lunch. Myron didn't get any information from her, and she didn't learn anything new. Well, that wasn't exactly true; his antipathy towards Javier was clear, and he seemed ready to throw Alicia under the bus, too. Even the food was unsatisfying, especially for the price. Thirty bucks for her mediocre lunch. The murals were wonderful, though, and the sorbet was good.

Bea told herself to quit having such mundane thoughts. They needed to clear this thing up, and fast. If Marcia really wanted her to help, then she needed to tell her more. That much was clear.

At least the monsoon clouds were building, she noticed.

* * *

That pleasant idea didn't last long. When Bea got back to work, she learned about another little plant offering. Someone had cut a few roses and laid them out in a bedraggled bunch in the lawn area. Javier had found the sad, dried-out flowers when he came in to work, but he had waited until he could talk to Angus about it. He'd figured it was just some stupid tourist who'd wanted to pick a few roses and then had gotten scared and left them. So, he'd cleaned them up and thrown them in the compost. The police took them out of the compost when Angus told Marcia about the incident. The thing was, tourists did pick flowers sometimes, when there wasn't anybody around. Bea had had to run after a woman with an armload of tulips once. So, Javier could have been right. Except that somebody, or somebodies, had been dropping so many little floral hints around the Gardens, and dead roses could be another one. The police checked the rose garden with Angus, and he said none of the roses had been recently cut.

Angus greeted her with this narrative when she got back to work. He thought Marcia was taking it seriously. It didn't look good for Javier that he didn't report the dead roses to the police. Javier got to the lawn area around 7:30, well before Shandley Gardens was open to the public. But there were grounds volunteers around by then; the weeding crew came in early on Tuesday mornings in the summer. They could have put the roses out, or more likely, they might have seen somebody sneak in and do it. The gate was open early on Tuesday mornings to let in the volunteers, and they figured if a stray tourist showed up that early and got in for free, it wasn't a huge deal. You wouldn't need a key to get in as you would have when somebody got the branch ready to fall on Saturday night or Sunday morning.

Surely the volunteers hadn't seen Javier do it. Bea couldn't ask anyone right then, because they'd gone home hours before by the time Javier told Angus about the situation, much less by the time Bea found out about it, post-luncheon.

Bea's cell phone rang. It was Marcia, of course. "Bea, I

need the phone numbers of your Tuesday weeding crew. Also, can you email me a report about your Cactus Club meeting?"

"Okay. Marcia, you don't really think Javier put those dead roses out on the lawn, do you? Because if he didn't report them, it's unlikely he was the one to put them out. I mean, if he was dropping some sort of nasty botanical message—if that's what you're thinking—he would have wanted people to see them!"

"Possibly. Unless the way he reported it was the way he wanted us to find out about them. The bottom line is that dead anything is not a good sign right now, Bea. I worked on a case where the murderer left a dead mouse by his victims' doors. It could be like that."

Bea shivered. She sure hoped nobody had it in for her. She'd just finished typing her latest report to Marcia when the office phone rang. It was the ubiquitous Dr. Joan Madsden, the plant sciences professor who enjoyed "playing in the dirt" as much as she enjoyed giving lectures.

"Bea, the oddest thing happened. Tell me if you think I should tell your policewoman friend."

Bea let out a half strangled "What?"

"I was heading over to the tool shed... around seven-forty-five or so, and there was this teenage girl, heavily made up so early in the morning, with a skin-tight tee shirt and shorts. She didn't look the type to get up early, and she certainly didn't look like the morning birdwatchers who know about the gate being open at seven-thirty on Tuesdays. Then I noticed she had a bunch of wilted roses, which she proceeded to drop onto the lawn. When she took off, I yelled at her and asked what the hell she thought she was doing. She yelled back, 'I'm making a weird-ass flower delivery.'"

"Thank God we know Javier didn't do it!"

"Bea, have you taken leave of your senses? Javier doesn't do things like *that*!"

"Joan, please call Detective Samuelson and tell her everything you just told me. Including what you said about Javier." She gave Joan Marcia's number.

"I'd be glad to call her. Especially if it helps Javier. Goodbye."

Well, maybe I helped that part of the investigation go faster. But I wonder who paid that girl to drop off the roses.

Bea walked out into swirling dust. If the parking lot hadn't been paved, it would have generated its own dust devil. The clouds she'd noticed at lunch were expanding across the sky. Maybe this would be it. Maybe it would rain and the murderer would be inspired to come clean.

But this was the most naïve kind of wishful thinking.

When she got home with the kids in her car there were dead yellow roses on her doorstep.

CHAPTER SEVENTEEN

Andy noticed them first when he got out of the car. "Wow, Mom, I sure hope nobody paid a lot for these flowers!"

He started to pick them up and Bea shouted at him, "Don't touch them!" He gave her a wide-eyed fearful look, and Jessie burst into tears. Bea hugged both kids and told them they didn't do anything wrong. She took them inside and broke her own rules, turning on a stupid TV comedy show, so she could make some calls. She left the roses right where they were.

The first was to Marcia, who said she'd be right over. The second was to Pat.

"You need to get them, Pat. Maybe for a couple of days. Please, no excuses. You know there has been a murder at Shandley, and now it looks like there may be some threat against me."

"Good God, Bea. I never thought you should work at that place. They don't pay you enough, and now it turns out the place is not safe for my kids. Yeah, I'll get them. I've found a neighbor who can pick them up from camp and take care of them when I'm not able to. And when their *mother* isn't able to." She wanted to respond to this, but she wasn't going to. The important thing was to keep the kids safe.

"Good, Pat. I'll see you shortly. I hope this is nothing. I hope Marcia solves this thing soon and we can all get back to normal."

"Marcia Samuelson?"

There was dislike in his voice. She remembered that tone; it meant he thought someone had wronged him. She wondered how Pat had gotten crosswise with Marcia, but it was not the time to ask, or even wonder about it.

* * *

When Pat knocked on Bea's door, Marcia was sitting in the living room. He gave her a careful neutral look, but then Jessie ran up to her father and flung her arms around him, saying, "Daddy, Mommy got some scary flowers."

Andy walked up more gradually and gave his dad a light hug. People said they looked alike, but Bea didn't see it beyond the red hair and green eyes. Pat was tall and trim with a direct, confident look. Andy was shy and rumpled.

He told his father, "The roses aren't scary, just all dried up, but the police want to look at them." He didn't like appearing vulnerable in front of Pat, maybe because his dad didn't approve of him being so shy. Maybe because he always had to be the big brother who knew more than Jessie. But his earlobe was red; he'd been pulling on it again.

Bea pulled him into her arms and said, "I love you. See you soon." Then she scooped Jessie in, too. She held them close and tried not to cry. When she let them go, Andy looked back just once, for a second. He pulled on his ear. She couldn't fully read the look, but there was worry in it. Was he concerned for her or just plain scared? Probably both. She had told him she wasn't in any danger. Would he lose trust in her?

Bea ran out to Pat's car as he was pulling away from the curb. She'd packed a few days of clothes for the kids. Who knew how long they'd have to be away?

Marcia's cell had rung during the goodbyes and she'd gone into the kitchen, where she was talking in a low voice. Bea went back inside as Pat's car disappeared from sight and started to clean cups off the coffee table because it was something to do, but she didn't know if she should take them to the kitchen. She stood there with several cups and glasses in each hand, feeling like an utter fool about hesitating to go into her own kitchen. Marcia walked through the kitchen door and Bea practically dropped all the dishes back onto the table, making a bigger mess than she'd started with.

"I'm really sorry to involve your kids in this, Bea. I'll do my damnedest to get your life back to normal." Marcia sighed. "Those roses do not appear to be from Shandley, either. Angus went out with one of our officers, and nothing has been cut. Angus says that neither bouquet is 'perfect' enough to be from a florist. Any ideas?"

"Well, the only person in our little group who I *know* grows roses is Buffy. But I haven't been to anybody else's houses, except Angus and Jean's, and Javier and Maria's. They do *not* grow roses. And by the way, Marcia, I meant to tell you: Javier saw Myron snooping around his house, looking over his fence a few days ago. Into their patio, where Maria makes her tile creations. Which, by the way don't look *anything* like those horrible portraits of Liz. Which I guess you must know."

Marcia gave a slight nod. "Thanks. We'll talk to Myron. And we'll send an officer around to Mrs. Jones's to have a look at her roses. I wonder why Javier didn't tell me about Myron's little visit?"

"Unlike some people around here, Javier doesn't traffic in character assassination. But he sent me over to talk to Maria, so he did let you know, in his way."

Marcia nodded again. She walked quickly into the kitchen... it was clear Bea wasn't supposed to follow her. When she returned to the living room, she said, "I'm going to have somebody tail you, Bea."

"Is that really necessary?"

"Let's just say you'd better keep safe for those kids."

Marcia knew she couldn't argue about that. "Now think hard, Bea. Is there any reason Buffy would have it in for you? And I imagine Myron would have access to her yard. What about him? Both of them just sought you out in ways they've never done before."

"I hardly know either of them. I'm just a staff member to them, a volunteer coordinator and educator. The only reason they paid any attention at all to me is that I know you. So maybe they're needling you by putting roses on my doorstep?"

"It's a possibility."

"Marcia, I just don't think it's Javier. Why would he want to bring the law down on himself? I don't mean he has anything to hide. He does have papers, and so does Maria."

"Yes, I know; we checked."

"I'm sure. But he might have friends who don't have papers. You know that as well as I do. He's not likely to want to shine the law's spotlight on his community. Plus..." *Steady Bea, you're getting emotional.* "Marcia, I just do not believe that Javier is a killer. I do not know Myron at all, so I can't say the same thing for him. But couldn't he be trying to frame Javier? Myron just inherited lots of money and now he can leave here and go to New York or San Francisco and be an artist, like he wants to."

"Yes, we're taking all that into consideration."

"Well, so what do you think? Are you getting close?"

"Maybe."

"Oh, come on."

"Bea, I don't see any advantage to telling you all of our thinking. For you or for us. The main thing now is to keep you safe. And for now, I wouldn't invite anybody over tonight."

Well, that took care of one potential issue. She had a night without the kids, but now she couldn't invite Frank over.

"Somebody will be watching your place. Let me know right away if you get any more information."

"Did you get a call from Joan Madsden? About seeing a girl drop off those roses at Shandley?"

"Yes, thanks for telling her to call me. We're looking into that. It may be the same person who delivered your bouquet. Take care."

Marcia left with those words. It seemed like she was expecting something, some clue to drop into place. Bea called Frank and told him about both sets of roses and the tail. He wanted to talk to her in person and cursed when she told him Marcia didn't want her to have anybody over.

"Okay, then. Let me tell you something else I found out. I've been doing a little digging on your boss. Do you know who paid his fines for the drug charge?"

"Who?"

"Mr. and Mrs. Gregory Jones. Now, I don't know why Buffy would do that for Ethan, way back twenty years ago, a long time before he was hired at Shandley. She was living here in Tucson, and he was way up in Flagstaff."

"Yeah, I know he got his bachelor's at Northern Arizona University, in Flag."

"Yup, he was in college when he got busted. It was for possession of psilocybin mushrooms. Ever the plantsman."

"If you found this out, I'll bet Marcia already knows."

"Why don't you tell her, just in case. And Bea... take care of yourself. I wish I could come over and make sure you're all right."

"Thanks, but Marcia's got some cop watching out for me."

Bea left a message on Marcia's cell about Ethan's fines. Then she found a piece of salmon in the freezer. The kids hated salmon; she wasn't sure why she had it, but she might as well do something to take advantage of this bizarre situation. She had put together a nice dinner of baked salmon, French bread, a green salad, and white wine, when her cell phone rang. She considered not answering it, but then she saw that it was Buffy.

"Bea, dear, how are you?"

"Well, honestly, I'm not too happy. Someone put some dead roses on my doorstep, and my kids had to leave the house for safety reasons."

"So *that's* why the police were in my garden today. They didn't do me the courtesy of explaining. They had a warrant, so there wasn't much I could do."

Here we go again. Pretending friendship when all she wants to do is pump me for information about what the cops are up to.

But Buffy was continuing. "I have something I'd like to show you, dear. Could you come over in the morning for a cup of coffee before work? Around eight or so?"

I suppose I can if someone is really watching me.

"All right. Buffy, can you tell me what this is about? I'm a little touchy lately, as you can probably imagine."

"Maybe I can help lessen your fears. Do come over."

"See you at eight."

Bea sat back in her chair and took three long breaths. Then she called Marcia, who assured her that she would not be alone. Marcia also said that the roses were *not* from Buffy's garden.

Bea heated up the salmon, ate her little dinner, drank the wine and called Andy and Jessie to wish them good night. "Are you okay, Mom?" asked her sensitive little guy. She assured him she was, poured another glass of wine, and tried to get some sleep.

She was not particularly successful at this. There was a long period, from about one to four a.m., when her mind was like a raft set out onto white water. She had dreamed of a multi-person shootout in Buffy's living room, with several people she didn't know. The bullets were flying everywhere but she couldn't see who had a gun. Then she stayed awake imagining more awful headlines about Shandley Gardens, needing to quit her job because of the craziness, being unemployed, and more dependent upon Pat. This was one of her more cheerful scenarios.

CHAPTER EIGHTEEN

Bea put an extra teaspoonful of coffee beans into the coffeemaker and managed to choke down a bit of whole-wheat toast with fig jam to accompany her huge mug of coffee. She found her white cotton dress, the most cooling thing she owned, and put on her white sandals. Blue enamel earrings to beckon the rain.

She noticed a black SUV that kept pace with her on the way to Buffy's. It wasn't Pat's car. It was somewhat comforting to be followed, but she was sweating more than made sense, even though it was another ridiculously hot June morning. *But* there was now a 50% chance of afternoon showers. They were edging closer to relief, at least as far as the weather went. Bea parked in Buffy's driveway and moved out of the car slowly. She noticed that at least one person was also getting out of the SUV, just beyond the driveway.

She rang Buffy's bell, and then she rang it again. She figured she'd ring it one more time, but then she noticed that the package leaning against the door had a card, and the card said "Bea." It was wrapped with expensive floral paper, and there was a note taped above the card. Bea didn't touch anything, but she scanned the note, written on torn yellow legal paper in spindly old-person's script: "Sorry I'm not here to give this to you, but I thought you'd appreciate this book, too." Bea felt like a fool, suspecting Buffy when she'd been kind to her... but still. She backed away from the door and then ran in the direction of the man who'd gotten out of the SUV. It turned out to be Officer Blake, partly obscured by a hedge. He told her to go on to work; he'd take care of the package. A police cruiser appeared and followed her to Shandley.

Of course, there was no way that Bea was going to be able to concentrate on anything. There was a volunteer meeting that morning. She walked in and said that something had come up, that she couldn't run the meeting. She asked the retired English professor prone to Shakespearean references to run it alone. Usually, they tag teamed it. There was some whispering when she left the meeting room, but mostly people looked genuinely concerned. On impulse, Bea walked back into the room. "As you know, this is a very tough time for the staff and board of Shandley. Thank you all so much for keeping the place running while we're so distracted. As always, we couldn't do it without you."

Good, one positive action for the day.

Bea called Marcia and asked if they'd opened the package. It was a book, only a book, about the language of flowers, a Victorian practice of saying things through flowers. Things you didn't want to say outright, in that far-off time when people were restrained about declaring their feelings. Marcia asked Bea to come down to the police station to look the book over with her. Bea was delighted to have an excuse to do something other than pretend to concentrate on most anything.

"Well, well, well," was the way Marcia greeted her. "We've had a lot of roses in this case. A lot of purposefully planted roses. So do you know what red roses symbolize?"

"Love, I would expect."

"Very good. And we've had some yellow ones, too. The rose between Liz's teeth on that first mosaic. And some in the dead bouquets. And at your doorstep."

"Do they mean jealousy?"

"They used to mean that, or infidelity. Except that florists nowadays want people to buy them so the new meanings are happiness and joy." She watched Bea for her reaction.

"The one on my doorstep wasn't a very joyful-looking bouquet," Bea said.

"We had pink roses in the bouquet on the lawn," Marcia continued.

"I think they mean friendship." Marcia nodded.

"Love, friendship, infidelity, jealousy, happiness, joy. A pretty full range of emotions."

Marcia just raised an eyebrow. "Okay, I'll try you on red tulips."

"Tell me. I don't know."

"They're a declaration of love. More love. Now we get to an interesting one. You remember that Liz was surrounded by datura in the second mosaic? The one on Buffy's porch?"

"Datura probably means something awful, since it's so toxic."

"It means 'beware.' And by the way, Bea, here's the card for you on Buffy's gift."

It was a photograph of white violets in the woods, blooming along a mountain stream. Inside the card, the barely legible, faltering cursive said, "I wanted to give you this book, as well. Buffy."

"White violets mean candor, and innocence."

"Oh, Marcia, she already gave me a book, and bookmarked a plate of white violets. And she was so sweet about it. I felt... well, I felt then, anyway, that she was reaching out to me. In a nice way. I'll bring you the first book."

Marcia said, "She does seem to be acting motherly towards you. Interesting."

Bea shook her head and put her hands up in a questioning gesture. "I don't know why I inspire that in her. So... is that it? Did we have any more floral messages?"

"Well, that's part of why I asked you to come down here. Have there been any other little botanical pieces to this puzzle that we've missed? That we don't know about?"

"Well, we are a botanical garden. We plant and water and deadhead and weed out flowers every day. I have no idea if any of our actions have a particular meaning." She thought a moment. "Maybe you should look up eucalyptus. The murder did occur in a eucalyptus grove."

"It's a good thing we have a modern version of *The Language of Flowers*. I doubt the Victorians were sending each other euke flowers." Marcia flipped through the book. "This says they mean 'protection.'"

"They weren't much protection for Liz."

"Somebody sawed through her protection."

"Okay, Marcia, stop playing games. Does this make any sense to you? Is this Buffy offering us help in some weird way? Or a confession of guilt, or what, for God's sake?"

Marcia was about to answer when Bea's cell phone rang. It was Frank. "Sorry, Marcia, I should have turned it off."

"Who is it?"

"Just this guy I've been seeing... a little of."

"The guy Frank who did some homework on Buffy and Liz when he was home visiting his mother?"

Of course, I typed up a whole report about that and emailed it to her. There are no secrets.

"Go ahead, Bea, take the call."

Frank was cautious. "Where are you right now?"

"At the police station. It's okay. I'm talking to Marcia. She's right here," she added, so he'd be careful about what he said on the phone. "I'll put you on speakerphone, okay?"

"Oh. Okay. Well, here's the thing. I got another call from the second woman I talked to—Penelope Locks—the one who knew Liz and Buffy at Davenport."

Bea looked up at Marcia. "And?"

"And another one of their old friends remembered that Buffy went down to the rainforest of the Yucatan on some volunteer project after she graduated from college. The group worked in the canopies looking for rare orchids. This murder is apparently the prime topic of interest among certain Davenport alumnae, who are all emailing each other about it, probably looking for some torrid tale related to the days of their youth."

"Yuck. Well, no wonder Buffy loves the tropical greenhouse."

"Yeah, that. Also, think about it. She was good at climbing trees."

"At eighty, Frank?"

"I don't know the woman, Bea. Anyway, I just wanted to report in."

"I'll talk to you later tonight. Thanks. I need to go."

When Bea hung up, Marcia said, "You might as well get back to your job, if you can concentrate."

"Fat chance of that. What are you going to do now?"

"I have a few things to check out."

"Are you keeping that book?"

"For now."

Bea had no choice but to go back to work. Ethan was now in his office. As she walked by, he asked her to come in. "How are you holding up, Bea?"

"I so much want this to be *over*. I think Marcia's close."

"That's a relief. I suppose I shouldn't ask you if I'm in trouble?"

"I don't think so, Ethan, but she doesn't tell me much. I'm sorry it's been so awful for you."

"Not just for me, for sure."

"True enough." Did Ethan think there was some reason he should be in trouble, or was he just worried and innocent, like she figured Javier was?

Then he asked her a surprising question. "Bea, did Armando mention that he was going plant collecting or anything to you?"

"No, he doesn't talk to me. But we're not supposed to leave the county."

"I know. But he's not answering his email or cell phone. He's not at work today, the department secretary said, and she said he missed a meeting."

"You should probably tell Marcia."

Ethan clearly didn't want to call Marcia, but he picked up his phone, and she left him to it.

What was Dr. Ramos up to now? Had he fled to Mexico? The Sonoran Desert he claimed to love extended down into the Mexican states of Sonora and Baja Norte. And what about Buffy and all the language of flowers hints? Bea asked herself the question that she noticed Marcia never answered, *Did Buffy plant the clues?* Bea kept coming back to the fact that Buffy might have been jealous that Liz stole her boyfriend, but that was decades and decades ago, and it surely seemed that they'd put their old friendship back together.

Buffy was genteel; it seemed more likely that giving Bea the book was her way of helping solve the murder. And Buffy seemed to feel closer to Bea than to Marcia, whose style was more hard-edged. Maybe Buffy knew the murderer was Myron, but she didn't want to accuse him directly. He sure had the best motive. Or maybe they were in it together.

That was awful, if it were true. The two of them, plus Liz, had seemed so close, a voting block, a social trio… Surely Myron and Buffy weren't secretly planning to do Liz in the whole time they hung out together.

Then there was Ethan, who *had* been acting strange. He was such a private person; when it came down to it, she knew almost nothing about him outside of his work persona. He surely knew the language of flowers. And Dr. Ramos probably did, too. Bea had no idea if Ramos could be violent or not, but he could be quite ill-natured. And if he really had a twisted mind, getting rid of Liz could help his faltering career. And maybe he'd gone into hiding!

The bottom line was, she didn't *really* know any of these people. Not well enough to understand what could make one of them to take the leap into something so deviant as murder. Somebody's mind had worked on a whole other circuit than the one most humans were plugged into, and that's why Bea had such a hard time understanding this whole thing.

Just as she was thinking about all of this, Marcia called. "We're looking for Buffy. As you suspected, she wasn't home when you came. Her car's not in the garage. We found something else for you when we searched the house. I'm going to scan it and email it to you. It was in the mailbox, which had the flag up."

That was all she said. The email followed shortly. It contained a letter:

"Bea, dear,

You saw me in the greenhouse and you asked if that was my favorite spot in the Gardens. I said, "Oh, yes." I love the beauty of the rainforest, the beauty of the orchids, and I was happy in the rainforest. I hope that you are able to find that kind of joy. I sense that you have had children to love in a way that I myself have never had. I am glad for you about that. I see in you my younger self—small but strong, loving flowers, bucking what's expected of you a bit.

I hope the book I gave you will help you discover what happened to Liz.

Buffy"

Why this letter? An idea began to germinate in Bea's brain.

CHAPTER NINETEEN

For once in her life, she'd been too distracted to notice the thunder. Then Angus burst in. He didn't even do his knocking code. "It's raining!" he said and did a little jig. She lost her train of thought and even forgot to look out the window at the rain, because Angus was a surprisingly great dancer.

As they turned together to her window, the spotty drops became a solid stream. Lightning singed the air and thunder shook the adobe walls. She could see a puddle... *an actual puddle* was forming on the walkway in the place where it dipped. Bea cracked her window to let in the rain-smells.

"I don't think there's a single floral perfume better than creosote bush in the rain," Angus said. "The closest creosotes were kind of far from our windows, so I put in a few for occasions like this."

"Thanks, Angus. It's like a good strong cup of coffee... it comforts while it stimulates."

They opened the window wider and stood there in silence. Bea's sandals were getting a little wet. "What's the likelihood of lightning coming through?" she asked.

"You have to take the risk," Angus said.

"Probably less than walking in the eucalyptus grove right now."

"Enough of that, Bea! Enough of climate change predictions of longer and hotter droughts, enough of this record-breaking year, enough of our damned little crew of possible murderers! The rains are here! Life is good."

"Smell it," she said. They were quiet again for a couple of minutes, taking deep breaths of the sweet-sagey smell of the plants, and listening to the battery of heavy rain drops on the tile roof.

"Angus, I think about leaving here, and working in a school, where I'd have better benefits and job security. But I can't do it. This is why. This, and watching which flowers are about to open and what's in fruit, and watching the agave stalks shoot up a foot overnight, and being able to walk out my door if I'm stressed to watch the lizards, and working with the volunteers on the fall and spring fiestas, and..."

"Yeah, I know. I know. Did you notice the night-blooming cereuses in the cactus garden are about to pop? You know they come out all together."

"Yeah. The Queens of the Night. And the closest I've been to seeing one bloom was the morning after. It had already wilted."

"Okay, I'll let you know when to come. You must not miss it. And Bea, I'll never leave unless they boot me out. But I'm not sure who 'they' is anymore. Who'll be running this place, when this is all done?" As he said this, the rain tapered back a bit, as if to emphasize his point.

"The only ones who really count are you and Javier. The rest of us could go away if necessary."

"Don't think like that. Shandley will pull through all this."

Suddenly a group of kids ran past their window, heading for the YMCA bus. The tour had been caught in the rain and had crowded into the meeting room until the rain let up; that was the monsoon procedure she'd given the tour guides. The kids would have had to squish in with everyone in the volunteer meeting, since there was only one big room at Shandley.

The guide waved at Bea and Angus as her group scurried by, laughing. Of course, no one had a raincoat. Some of them probably didn't even own one.

"I should head back to work," said Angus.

"Not yet. I have to tell you about Buffy's letter."

He nodded and sat down. She read the letter from her computer screen.

"Well, that's curious, all right," Angus said. "You know, I've seen Buffy moping around the tropical greenhouse a lot lately. And another time, we were sitting on a garden bench, looking at a seed catalog. She wanted some advice for her garden. So she suddenly asked me if I had any kids, and I said no, and she said that sometimes it was hard to forget something 'terribly sad' that had happened to her and made her unable to have kids. So then when I said Jean and I'd planned it that way she looked surprised. The whole thing was bizarre. So, I can't say *I'm* surprised by Buffy's vision of you as the woman she wished she'd been."

"Okay, Angus, that's not all. She left a copy of *The Language of Flowers* for me on her front doorstep. Marcia thinks all the roses and tulips and datura and things are messages."

"Like the Victorians? Well, she is kind of Victorian."

"If she's the one who left the clues."

"Ah, yes, there is that."

"And now nobody knows where she or Dr. Ramos is."

"*That's* an unlikely pair. I can't see the two of them running off to Mexico together."

Bea had an idea about running off to Mexico that she was going to run by Angus, but he cut her off.

"I'd better get back to work, Bea, and see what damage the storm did. I want to make sure I'm not responsible for any more hazards to the public. I'm going to check the eucalyptus grove right now. Did you hear that *crack!* when the lightning was close?

"Oh, Lord, not again!"

"I hope not. But assuming there are no new crises, I'll try to focus on everything you just told me. I think better when my hands are doing something."

Angus left and Bea shook her head to clear it of the stuff that was gumming up her brain. It was monsooning, after all.

"Now you just have to cheer up, Cassandra!" It was Dr. Madsden, peering in her door. "All is well in the Sonoran Desert!"

"Mostly," said Bea, but Dr. Madsden did not look satisfied. When she left, Bea squared her shoulders and gave Marcia a call. She ran a crazy idea by her. Marcia was noncommittal, as usual.

And so, Bea felt free to relax into the late afternoon's work. She was scheduled to give a presentation at a meeting of a homeowners' association. They were thinking of ripping out their grass. They'd been humiliated by the same article that called Shandley out for its water use. *Oh, yeah, that's where all this started. Getting rid of the lawn for the Events Center.*

The rain seemed to have brought Dr. Ramos back from wherever he'd been. Bea's door was open, and she heard him mutter, "police state." Then he stood in the hallway and yelled. "Officer, I wasn't very far outside the county limits, for God's sake." She took a quick look out her door. He was on his cell. There was a pause after his outburst. Then he said, only slightly less aggressively, "Do you want to see my full plant presses as evidence?"

He always had full plant presses in the back of his truck. She supposed she'd have to tell Marcia that. She was getting sick of being a snitch.

She heard Ramos's footsteps heading towards the front of the building. She headed towards the front door herself, thinking her excuse would be to get a granola bar out of the car.

Dr. Ramos was off the phone and angrily slamming the camper door of his pickup. He turned towards her and exploded.

"Don't think I don't see your hand in this persecution, Missy. It's a sorry situation when an employee like you has influence on the cops."

"You're entirely wrong, Dr. Ramos. Detective Samuelson makes all of her own judgments and keeps her conclusions to herself." Bea was pleased at what sounded like rational words coming out of her mouth. *Missy indeed.*

"The board will have something to say about your behavior once this whole thing is over."

"Dr. Ramos, Ethan is my supervisor."

"Well, we'll see where this investigation leaves him, won't we?"

"I guess we will." She smiled at him pointedly. *Now I*

really will tell Marcia about the plant presses he keeps in his truck 24/7.

When Bea got Marcia on the line, she let out a long exhalation. She waited a moment before saying, "Thanks, Bea. I'm not surprised. We'll have to see if the plants have been collected in the last few hours. I imagine we can figure that out. I wonder if he's collecting datura."

"He seems to think I have an unfair influence on you. He called me Missy."

"You have a pretty fair influence on me, Missy."

Marcia clearly didn't like Dr. Ramos, but Bea couldn't tell if he was a serious suspect.

* * *

By the time she headed home, the sun was out again. But the air was thirty degrees cooler. And there was rain in the forecast for the next day. The water bottle she always kept in the front seat had lukewarm, actually drinkable water in it, instead of being the right temperature for a tea bag. The birds were singing with their own post-monsoon elation, and the dust that had covered the city like a brown snowfall had now washed right down the street drains.

Marcia had called to say that Bea would have a different tail that evening. He'd be in a blue sedan and he'd park outside her unit. They'd catch up later.

"Is there still a ban on having someone over this evening?"

"Your sleuthing friend?"

"I'm considering inviting him for dinner."

"Sure, if you want to do that."

Her kids were still at Pat's. She called to make sure everything was okay, and Andy told her that "Mrs. Johnson" had picked them up from school and was going to "watch" them until their dad came home after dinner. Well, she was glad that he had found Mrs. Johnson. Maybe she would enable Pat to keep his commitments. Now she could invite Frank over for dinner, just the two of them. Would she do this because she really wanted his company, or because she was afraid to be alone after all this drama? It was probably for both reasons. Maybe if she told him up front that he couldn't spend the night, the situation would feel less fraught.

"Hey, Frank. Would you like to come over for dinner? And I'm asking you just for dinner."

He chuckled. "Sure. Are you okay? Are you still under surveillance?"

"Yeah. But things are better. It rained, right? I can catch you up this evening. I've got veggie burgers with cheese, some little potatoes to roast, and salad."

"Kid food. How about if I take you out to Mario's? I just got a decent check in today's mail."

Mario's advertised "fine Italian dining." That sounded wonderful to Bea at that moment.

The blue sedan followed them to Mario's.

The pasta puttanesca and sangiovese loosened her tongue. She told him that she hoped Marcia had found Buffy. Surely there was a reason she'd left the house that didn't involve being guilty of murder. Bea realized she didn't want Buffy to go to jail. She also didn't want Buffy to have disappeared because of someone else's dastardly deed. The letter from the older woman had touched her.

Then she and Frank began speculating about who might have gone to all the trouble of leaving the floral clues.

"Bea, what color were the roses on your doorstep? What was this person trying to say to you?"

"They were yellow. Yellow roses confuse me. They meant jealousy or infidelity in Victorian times, but now the florists want to sell them, so they seem to mean affection, happiness and joy. So, I'm not sure what someone was trying to say to me. Although I suspect the jealousy meaning. It wasn't a pretty bouquet, believe me."

"Let's go for happiness, affection, and joy." He was flirting with her. It felt kind of fun.

"Yes, let's."

She was looking at Frank, but somewhere in the periphery she caught sight of a familiar figure in the doorway facing her. Dr. Ramos walked into Mario's, accompanied by a very young Latina. Bea sincerely hoped it wasn't one of his students, because he cupped her ass briefly. The uncommonly pretty young woman gave him a warning look, which Bea noticed.

It seemed time to ask for the check. But as Bea looked for the waiter, she saw the next arrivals at the restaurant. Alicia and Raoul Vargas walked through the door, waved at Dr. Ramos and the young woman, and proceeded to their table. The Vargases sat down with the couple. It looked like they were going to dine together. Bea had no idea the Vargases socialized with Armando outside of board events. Was this a nefarious meeting that had something to do with the murder? Should she go over and say hello, or pretend she hadn't seen them, and ask Frank to leave with her quickly? He still didn't know who'd come in. They probably didn't see Bea because her table was angled in a way that gave the others a good view only of Frank, whom they didn't know.

She told Frank she had to go to the rest room. He gave her a questioning look; she was clearly distracted and had broken off their convivial conversation. The rest room was behind the board members' table, so she walked directly by them, pretending that she hadn't known they were all sitting there.

She managed to hear Dr. Ramos saying something about endowment being essential before she had to announce herself. "Oh, hi!" she said in a startled way.

Alicia sensed her surprise about this social gathering. "Bea, meet our daughter, Catalina."

Bea really *was* taken aback this time, but now she had to pretend not to be shocked. "So nice to meet you," she said, extending her hand.

Catalina was more than pretty. She had huge brown eyes and a smile that stunned. Bea sincerely hoped this romance was short-lived. She would have to admit that Dr. Ramos was handsome, if you managed to ignore his personality. But he was practically as old as Catalina's father, which she could see clearly, as they were seated next to each other. She caught Raoul Vargas watching Armando very carefully, and she decided she wasn't the only one disturbed about Catalina's relationship with Armando Ramos.

"Good to see you all. I'm just headed to the restroom," she said, realizing how lame that sounded.

Of course, Ramos couldn't just let her go without a jab. "Little Miss Detective is at it at all hours, I see."

To her credit, Catalina looked shocked. Her mother quickly interjected, "I hope you can help us get this over with as soon as possible, Bea. Thank you for helping the police."

"You're welcome," Bea said. She looked at Alicia and then Raoul when she said it, and pointedly ignored Ramos. As she headed for the rest room, she mused that she should join a cloister so she could get away from the males of the species. But she couldn't have her kids with her then, besides the fact that she wasn't Catholic and wasn't even very religious. And, of course, she'd hate being a nun.

There were a few problems with this scenario, granted. She wasn't really being fair, lumping Frank in with Armando and Pat.

She got back to the table and explained to Frank who composed the foursome across the room. "How about we get out of here and head to a gelato bar for dessert?" she said.

Frank's head sagged a bit and she suspected he was sad that the mood between them had broken. She didn't blame him. She would have loved the tiramisu and grappa they'd talked about, and a little more flirtation, but that was not to be, this time.

But Frank wasn't about to let the evening devolve into the mundane. "That gelato place is full of college kids. I understand why you want to leave here, but let's get a tiramisu to go, and we can eat it in the Foothills Park. The stars are nice out there, and I'll pick up a little bottle of grappa to celebrate selling that short story."

"That sounds a lot better than the gelato bar."

Bea waved to the board members on the way out. Catalina called out, "Nice to meet you, Bea!" prompting a startled look from her date.

The park was mostly desert vegetation, with a few covered picnic tables. They sat out in the patch of grass. "A little goes a long way." She was talking about the grass, but she was thinking it applied to the grappa. And a kind man who seemed to support who she was.

Her cell phone rang. She wanted to ignore it. But what if it was about the kids? More likely, it was Marcia. She looked at the phone for a second. It was an unknown number. Not worth answering right now. It had rained a lot up in the foothills, and there was the rich smell of dry grass that had just been soaked. She was starting to relax.

The phone beeped with notice of a voice mail.

"Bea, it's okay if you need to get it."

"I don't want to."

"It's up to you. It'll still be a beautiful night out here when you get off the phone. On the other hand, it's a beautiful night right now." He stroked her arm once.

She sighed and pulled out her phone to listen to the message.

It was Angus, calling from his home phone. That's why she hadn't recognized the number. She pressed *call back*.

"Are you sitting down?"

"Very much so." She smiled at Frank.

"I was just hanging out with some old plant nerd friends who know Armando. He definitely wasn't collecting plants this afternoon."

"Nor this evening. He was at Mario's, and he was sitting with the Vargases."

"*That* surprises me. Well, don't you want to know where he was earlier?"

"Tell me. I'm on a date, I guess, and I don't want to talk long."

Frank chuckled.

"Date, huh? Well, our buddy Armando was collecting information this afternoon, not plants. He called around to the horticulture community to announce Ethan's old drug bust, and was talking trash about Ethan to everybody, implying that he was an unethical S.O.B. My friend Lew said he was implying that he'd make a much better director than Ethan.

For sure he was looking for dirt on Ethan, to tell Marcia, maybe, or the board. So much for being Ethan's jogging buddy."

"Maybe Dr. Ramos figures he can get the director job rather than the new job he's trying to get Ethan to create. I hope I don't ever figure into his schemes." She wondered how Catalina did. She looked over at Frank, who was watching her face. "Angus, I'll talk to you tomorrow."

"Sorry to interrupt whatever's happening."

"Don't be."

She got off the phone and sighed. Frank offered her a sip of grappa.

"I don't even want to talk about what that was about. Let's see which constellations we can name."

They made it through the Big Dipper, Sagittarius, and Leo. After that, words were excess baggage. Frank's touch was gentle. Bea didn't invite him back to her place, but she certainly thought about it.

CHAPTER TWENTY

The next morning, Bea didn't have to take the kids anywhere, no lunches to make, and no shoes to find. She'd set the alarm for 8:15 to get to work by 9:00, but years of accommodating the sleep habits of small children kept her from her plan. She was wide-eyed when her cell phone rang at 7:30. This time she recognized the number. She had hoped it was Frank, but it was the Shandley number, and it was her boss.

"Bea, are you sitting down?"

Not this again. "Yes. I hope this is not something horrible."

"No. Well, yes, in some ways. Buffy killed herself. She left a suicide note that tells everything. It's incredibly complicated, and I need a little time to digest it all. The good part is, it's over. For now, just relax. Take the day off. The media will be all over Shandley again. Take it with pay. You deserve it. I'm sorry this has been so tough on you and your kids."

"You're not going to tell me any more than that?"

"Bea, I'm still processing the whole thing. I've been awake all night. You're not in trouble with the law, and neither am I. That's enough for now, right? I promise you'll learn more soon."

"Who found Buffy? Where was she?"

"She went out into the desert, to a little cave in the Rincons. She poisoned herself. The Park Service noticed her car was in a day hiking lot overnight. A ranger had seen an elderly, frail woman laboring up the trail yesterday. When her car was still there after dark, another ranger followed her footprints. She was already gone when he got to the cave."

"That makes me sad. But I'm incredibly relieved that it's over. Can you swear to me that it's over?"

"It's over, I swear."

"Are Javier and Maria in the clear? And Angus?"

"Yes."

"And… I guess I want to know if the Vargases are in the clear. So many people… well, the media anyway… thought they couldn't possibly have ignored all those slights from the Shandleys. But was Alicia really just being professional?"

"Yes, of course, Bea." He sounded almost scolding about that, but then he came back to being overwhelmed.

"Bea, I have to get my head around this. I promise you'll know everything you want to know soon."

"Okay, I can live with that."

"Have a good day."

She had no doubt that she could comply with that order from her boss.

"I will. And thanks for telling me, Ethan." He was a good guy. She'd thought so and was sorry she'd ever doubted him. It was a little frustrating to be left with such partial information, but hey, it was good partial information. And it fit with what she'd been thinking.

What did she want to do with a whole day off, and no kids? *Not* clean the house, which was her usual go-to activity, but only because it was direly needed. She hated cleaning house, and she was not about to do it today.

She called Frank and asked him if he could take a day off from work.

"I can. I'm surprised you can. Did you decide you needed to call in sick to think things through?"

She told him what Ethan had said. "Why don't you come over here for breakfast, and we can go from there?" she asked.

* * *

Breakfast was kind of like counting constellations the night before. The scrambled eggs looked good, but they were superfluous. This time she was sure about inviting him into her bed.

It had rained, the crime was solved, Javier was okay, Maria was okay. Cause for celebration. There was a call from Marcia and Bea did something that felt really good. She ignored it.

It may have been good luck that brought Bea and Frank together in the first place at that potluck, and it may have been good luck that they had a free day together when the crime was solved, but it was more than luck that happened that morning. It was also more than lust.

Lying in bed way late into the morning, Bea found herself reflexively listening for sounds of children coughing, or crying, or playing. *Everything is surreal. I'm back in my dating days. Somehow the murder is solved, although there's something so odd about it that Ethan can't even tell me.* She ran her fingers through Frank's chest hair, and he picked them up and kissed each finger. It was another hour before she threw open the curtains, to the strains of Mozart's Jupiter symphony.

Since it was now lunchtime, they rolled their uneaten eggs into tortillas, ladled them with salsa, and cut pieces of every fruit she had in the house—mangoes, strawberries, and oranges. The oranges were from Frank's tree, and they abandoned the other fruits and fed each other orange slices. Between slices, Bea told Frank her crazy ideas about what they might hear from Ethan.

"I look forward to finding out how crazy you are. Maybe not so much," he said.

The phone rang. Marcia again, and time to answer it.

"Bea, I know Ethan told you the bare essentials, and I know he wants to explain the rest in his own way. But we've talked to the media, and the story's coming out, so I wanted to connect with you, to make sure you know what we told the media. And to thank you. You helped us solve this a lot faster."

"Thanks. So, this is all very mysterious, but tell me what you will."

"Buffy killed Liz. Buffy had terminal lung cancer. That's

why you thought she looked so thin and unhealthy. She left a suicide note for the public, and a different one that Ethan will read to the staff later. The public suicide note explains that she had always loved Alan Shandley, and had been jealous of his marriage to Liz. She killed Liz out of jealousy, then killed herself."

"How did she kill herself?" How bizarre to be asking this question as if she were asking about yesterday's rainfall total.

"As you might expect, botanically. She made a strong brew of oleander leaves. She could have picked it off a bush on practically any street in the old part of Tucson, as you know. I looked up oleander in the *Language of Flowers*. It means 'beware.' It's a common suicide method in Sri Lanka."

"She probably traveled there. It's pretty tropical." *What an inane thing to say*. But what could she possibly say that *was* appropriate?

"Ethan asked to tell the staff the rest, so you'll have to wait until you go into work tomorrow. I suspect you won't be entirely surprised."

"Well, okay," she said, but it was frustrating.

"Let's not let *that* ruin the day," she said, when she explained Marcia's call to Frank. They were planning some museum-hopping when the camp director called. Jessie had twisted her ankle playing soccer, and the guy said it ought to be X-rayed to make sure it wasn't broken. Pat was officially on kid duty, of course, but Bea wanted to be the one who took her to urgent care, rather than Pat's babysitter.

"I'm sorry, Frank. Please don't feel like you need to help us do this."

"Well, Bea, I didn't want to mention it, but I do have another deadline. I was just going to stay up late tonight."

"Go ahead. We have plenty of time to go to museums. Plenty of time to do all sorts of stuff." She'd forgotten what it felt like to look forward to being with someone in this way.

Nothing was going to shake her good mood. Not even a three-hour wait in urgent care, because no one there seemed to think Jessie had much of an emergency. They were right;

she was sent home with an Ace bandage and instructions about icing and elevating her "minor" sprain. Jessie was delighted because she was home alone with her mom and the doctor's instructions meant she could spend the afternoon watching television, which was an unheard-of dispensation.

Bea called Pat about Jessie's non-injury and said she'd pick Andy up at the bus stop. "This whole thing is almost over, Pat. It'll be in the news. I'll talk to you about it soon."

"Thank God, Bea. I'll let Mrs. Johnson know she doesn't have to go to your bus stop to get Andy. And I'll wait to hear more from you. You're being kind of mysterious."

Because my boss is being mysterious. But she wouldn't say that to Pat.

As Bea was getting Jessie ready to pick up Andy, thunder shook the house briefly. Bea looked out the window and saw the rain curtain was closing in. Then the thunder was nearly on top of them, and the lightning was close enough to require a run for the car. As they drove, the car sloshed through streets flowing with runoff. Bea felt as if she were dodging lightning bolts in the few-blocks drive, as she sang "Let it rain, let it pour, let it rain a whole lot more!" at the top of her lungs. So what if there weren't enough drains in Tucson, at least she didn't have to go through a flooded wash to get to the bus.

"Mama, I'm cold," said Jessie.

"I'll bet you forgot what cold is."

"Yeah, kinda. Mommy, I kinda like being cold."

On the way back home, she belted out the gospel tune, "The storm is passing over, Allelu." Andy joined her on the chorus. This was their monsoon ritual song, which he'd remembered from last summer.

"Wow, Mom, can we go out after this is over and see if there are any tarantulas out?" he asked when she took a breath.

"You bet." And sure enough, Andy found one; the males often came out to search for mates after a rainstorm. The females waited in their burrows. Humans weren't the only ones to appreciate monsoons.

Bea hoped it was a long, wild, monsoon season, with plenty of thunder, lots of lightning that didn't start any wildfires, and enough rain to revive all the spindly plants and turn the desert floor green.

CHAPTER TWENTY-ONE

There was no reason to skip her morning meditation. The news media had had a field day yesterday, but the parking lot that morning was empty of any cars but the staff's. Bea took three lung-filling breaths. The big spiny golden barrels, the prickly pears, the aloes, the saguaros that stretched all the way to the mountains... was it her imagination, or had these succulent plants already plumped up from yesterday's rains? She caught up with Angus on the way in the door.

"Tonight's the night for the night-blooming cereus. The Queen of the Night will show her full glory tonight, Bea. You should bring your kids and come back and see them. We've got four plants about to pop."

Ethan had called an all-staff meeting for 10:00. Bea, Angus, and Javier—their whole tiny staff—filed into the meeting room, hushed and expectant. They'd caught sight of their boss already and could see he'd lost the tense look he'd had for the last few days.

"As I told each of you on the phone, there was more in Buffy's suicide letter than the media reported. It was more than a letter. It was practically a short memoir. Myron has asked that the contents be sealed to the public, and the police see no reason that his request should not be honored." He took a breath. "It's a little hard to explain this, but I want you three to know, and Myron agrees." He took another breath.

"As you all may know, given all the gossip around this case, Buffy and Alan dated when she was in high school."

Bea nodded and Angus nodded beside her. She wondered where Ethan was going with this.

"So you did all know that," he said. "You may know this next part, too. Liz went to college in the Boston area. Buffy went to her mother's alma mater, which was in California. Alan was in the Air Force part of the time they were in college, but when he got out he went to Harvard. Near Liz." So far, there was nothing new to Bea in this account. "Apparently, Liz and Alan starting dating. Then Liz got pregnant, and they got married."

"She got pregnant with Myron?" Angus asked.

"No. Liz lost this baby, and she was unable to have another child."

"Her, too?" said Angus.

Ethan looked down at his hands for a moment and continued in an even tone. "In the meantime, Buffy was at Evans College, in the Bay Area, recovering from what she felt was a terrible betrayal. She graduated from Evans in botany after the war was over, and did some field work in the Yucatan. She was up on tree canopy platforms, collecting orchids. She was proud of 'bucking the norms' for women in the late forties. About this time, Alan started collecting plants. He took a long expedition to Mexico, which included time in the Yucatan."

"Uh-oh," said Angus.

"Exactly. Buffy became pregnant."

"With Myron. Am I right?" Bea asked. Ethan nodded. Angus stared at her.

Bea continued, "Liz couldn't have kids, Buffy could. But Buffy told Angus she couldn't 'have' kids, which made her so sad. That's because she gave Myron up for adoption. To Liz and Alan. So incredibly bizarre."

"Yes, Bea, you got it. I sure didn't. The thing is, you have to remember this was not a time when society, especially Buffy's branch of it, looked well on single mothers. Her parents sent her to some discreet place in Pennsylvania where wealthy young ladies sewed and read and gave their babies up and went on with their lives afterwards. According to her letter, she 'succumbed to convention.' She re-entered Philadelphia society, and a couple of years later, married Greg

Jones, an up-and-coming young businessman, a Chamber of Commerce member. They settled in the neighborhood where she grew up, and, she said, 'she tried hard to fulfill the role of a proper wife.'"

"It seems like you have this 'memoir' down, Ethan," said Angus.

"Yeah, I've read it over many times since Myron gave me a copy yesterday."

"So, Ethan, how did Myron end up with Liz and Alan? That part's hard to figure," Bea said.

Ethan took another breath. "This is where it starts to get... unusual. Buffy placed the baby with an adoption agency. She told Alan ahead of time the name of the agency, and of course they knew the approximate due date. Somehow Alan convinced Liz to adopt the baby. Liz was unable to have children after her first failed pregnancy. The baby's birth parents were undisclosed to the adoptive parents; that was not uncommon in those days.

"Did Liz ever know?" asked Angus.

"According to Buffy, no. Myron didn't really look like his father, other than his height; that helped. He didn't act much like him, either."

Angus could only reply with "wow," but Javier had more to say. He'd been twisting his hands together during the last part of Ethan's story, and he said, "I always thought so. I knew Alan and Mrs. Jones cared for each other. I saw... never mind what I saw. And she cared so much for Myron, too."

"She wanted a child so badly," said Bea.

Ethan looked at her. "Well, she had one."

"I'll bet Myron knew he was her son. I think that's why they seemed so close when Angus ran into them on the bench," Bea said.

Ethan squinted at her. "I don't know what you're talking about. But the bottom line is, most of Myron's life he didn't know. His parents never told him that he was adopted, which is odd, but not as uncommon for earlier generations." Ethan's gaze wandered to the mesquite trees framed by the meeting room window. He turned back to them and continued in a resolute tone. "Meanwhile, Liz and Alan were living in the Boston area, but Alan was restless. As a child, he'd spent his summers at a ranch in Colorado, and he loved the Southwest. He'd been trained in Tucson at the army air field in World War II, and he'd fallen for the desert. So, he wanted to head west and try his fortune in Tucson. Liz, as you probably remember, was not much of an adventurer."

Angus snorted and then studied his fingernails. Ethan looked at him a moment, and continued, "Buffy wrote that Liz 'resisted the move mightily,' but, like Buffy, she was a good fifties housewife, so she gave in. They moved to Tucson, which Alan rightly thought would attract plenty of people because of its desert climate. They got into the real estate business in the early fifties. You know, the population almost quadrupled from 1950 to 1960. Alan's timing was perfect.

"Back to Buffy. Greg Jones wanted to go west, too. Buffy convinced him to head to Tucson. She was still carrying a torch for Alan, apparently. They arrived a few years after the Shandleys."

"Uh oh, again," said Angus.

"Yes. Well. The Shandleys and the Joneses were in the same social set, and they seemed to get along fine as a four-some. Water under the bridge. They rode horses into the desert together, took picnics in the mountains. But Buffy said 'My heart was broken again, because Alan would not leave Liz. The real reason she stayed close with the Shandleys was to watch Myron grow up."

"God, poor Myron. So, did he know by this time? Did he suspect?" asked Angus.

"Myron and I had a long talk yesterday. It was only fairly recently that he really suspected. Buffy was acting unusu-ally proprietary. He'd always felt a kinship with her, and he'd always noticed their eyes. Have you noticed their eyes?"

"Yes. Gray. Kind of an almond shape," Bea said.

"I never noticed," said Angus.

"Me either, but there it is," said Ethan. "So Myron asked her if she was his mother, just a few days ago, and she admit-ted that she was."

"So yeah, Bea, I'll bet you're right. That was the moment, on the bench. A few days ago. When I watched them fall into each other's arms, crying." said Angus.

Ethan gave him a sharp look. Even now he seemed to think it was unethical to spy on board members. He continued, "Myron was worried that Buffy had killed Liz out of jealousy. She had told him of her tree-climbing past; he knew about that. But she didn't admit to the murder... not until we got this letter."

"So that's why he started to look so wan," said Angus.

"And why he tried to throw shade on all kinds of other people when he took me to lunch at the Cactus Club."

Angus cut in. "When Liz died, at first he seemed sad, but then he was striding around in a way I'd never seen before. Like maybe he was liberated. But then he got more and more pale and worried." Ethan wasn't going to be able to stop Angus from these musings.

"Myron cared very much about Buffy," Ethan continued. "When he found out she was his mother, he was relieved. There was always tension between him and Liz. He felt guilty that he wasn't a good son to her, and I think she fed that guilt. Buffy said that since he couldn't satisfy his father's ambitions for him, he satisfied his mother's by being a pillar of Tucson society. Buffy implied he didn't like that either, but who knows if that's really the case."

"God, do you suppose Liz suspected all this stuff? Did she notice their eyes? I mean, if Bea saw the similarities...?" asked Angus.

Bea said nothing. Liz and Buffy and Myron had appeared to be such a tight trio. She hadn't noticed tension between Myron and Liz. It was easy to be blind to the inner dynamics of other people, though. And before this all happened, she hadn't been watching the board members all that closely. She hadn't needed to. What if Liz had been taking her suspicions out on her son, his whole lifetime? What if she'd tortured her husband with her mistrust? Fortunately, she'd never know those details.

"So," she said, "Myron wanted to divert attention from

Buffy. That's why he tried to convince everybody it was you, Javier. He was checking out your patio to build a case against you and Maria."

Javier looked up. "He might have been Alan's son, but he was not like Alan."

"Which is probably why Alan so respected you. You *were* like him," she said.

"Yes."

"This is such a strange tale. But there's something I still don't get. Why did Buffy kill Liz *now*? I mean, Myron's how old? Fifty-nine?" Angus asked.

"Yeah, this story has been going on for a very long time. And it's far from over," Ethan said.

"Lord help us," said Angus.

"So." Ethan paused. "You never know what really goes on between two people."

You took the thought right out of my head. Javier met her eyes. He'd been saying that to her.

Ethan continued: "Or four people, in this case. Buffy said she and Greg had a strained marriage. They were unable to have kids. She knew it wasn't her issue, because of Myron, but she never told Greg about that. She got tested, and of course she was fertile. She finally got him to agree to get tested, and sure enough, he had an extremely low sperm count. By that time, he'd decided he liked their comfortable life and didn't want to add kids into the mix. Buffy took a long trip to South Africa, working as a volunteer at a botanical preserve. At some point, Alan was down there on another collecting trip."

"Uh-oh, for the third time," said Angus.

I'm not going to mention this, but Greg and Buffy Jones helped Ethan when he got busted. And Ethan's small and neat like Buffy. But he's about to tell us what I've been suspecting, Bea thought.

Ethan looked down at his hands for a moment. He took a deep breath, and expelled it as he raised his head and looked at his three staff members.

"I'm Buffy and Alan's second son."

"No way!" Angus yelled.

"I just found this out yesterday. I'm more surprised than you are."

"Let me get this straight," Bea said. "Buffy got pregnant and her husband knew it wasn't his child because he was sterile, or because he wasn't around Buffy at the time of conception, or both."

"Yes."

"So did she go off to some unwed mothers' place again?" Bea asked. "And then when your parents adopted you... you grew up in northern Arizona, right?" He nodded, looking a little stunned." Bea said more gently, "She followed your life somehow and knew you were a plantsman?" Ethan just nodded, looking down at his hands. She didn't add that then Buffy was on the hiring committee, making sure he took over where his father had left off at Shandley Gardens.

"You're almost right on, Bea. Greg agreed not to divorce her if she gave up the baby. Me. They went off to Canada for the last few months of the pregnancy. I guess he made up some business excuse. The story was that she lost the baby. Even her parents thought it was stillborn."

"I heard she'd had some tragedy like that," Javier commented.

"It was a closed adoption, again." Bea said. "The records were sealed. But somehow Buffy followed your life."

"Yes," Ethan said. "She knew where I went to elementary school in Winslow, Arizona. She knew I went to Northern Arizona University for both my bachelor's and my master's. Somehow, she knew that I hadn't had a very warm childhood; I was an only child of two parents who adopted me because all their friends had children, and it was expected of them. One was enough for them, believe me." Ethan grimaced at some unpleasant memory.

"Anyway, Buffy wrote that watching out for me was her way of assuaging her guilt." He stopped for a minute and sighed. He'd been saying this with his eyes downcast most of the time, looking up every so often at the end of a sentence. Then he looked straight at them. "So she paid my fines when I was stupid enough to get caught with some psilocybin mushrooms. That was the first time I'd heard of Mrs. Gregory Jones, and I always wondered who she was and why she did that. I tried to thank her, but I wasn't given any contact information. I just gave a letter to my lawyer."

Bea and Angus exchanged a quick glance.

"You can imagine my surprise when there was a Mrs. Gregory Jones on the hiring committee for this job. Of course, the felony was right there on the application, so I asked her in private if she was the person who paid my fines. She never told me she was my mother, just like she never told Myron. She just said she made a habit of helping promising young people. The difference between me and Myron is that I never suspected."

Bea had been looking at him during this recitation. He did *not* have those gray, almond-shaped eyes. His eyes were large and brown. He probably looked like a smaller version of Alan, who'd died long before she came to the Gardens. But he also looked like Myron's younger, shorter, fitter, healthier brother. She'd remarked on their resemblance, in their dark suits, seated on either side of Buffy at Liz's memorial service. It wasn't an illusion.

Bea had gotten this far in her private musings. She'd thought Myron was Buffy's son, and maybe, in a long shot, Ethan, too. She'd even thought that maybe Buffy killed herself because she was dying... all those pill bottles at her house... and she didn't want go on trial for killing Liz in her last days. That part made sense. But for God's sake, why kill Liz now?

She said, "Buffy kept this secret until she died. She killed Liz because she wanted to give her sons the truth, and Liz couldn't be alive to hear it?"

Ethan let out a ragged sigh. "I'm going to read you the last part of the letter from my... mother." He looked at the floor once more when he said that, and they all followed his eyes, thinking that maybe the letter was down there. But he was just trying to solidify that word "mother," Bea thought, by looking at the floor.

Then he pulled several photocopied pages out of his shirt

pocket. They'd been folded and unfolded numerous times. It was hard to believe he'd gotten this copy only the day before. He started reading one of the last pages.

"My dear sons, I suppose you'll wonder why I waited to tell you all this now, and why, after all these years, I killed my friend Liz. It's very simple, really. I couldn't tell you while she was alive. And Liz's death frees you both to be who you want to be. Myron, I know that you feel, out of some exaggerated sense of filial duty, that you must shoulder your parents' charge of carrying on both the family business and Shandley Gardens. Liz fed that guilt, as you know all too well. Ethan, you are now taking on your father's work at Shandley, the work of his heart, and I can see that it is the work of your heart, too. You probably know that Liz was never a big supporter of yours, and that she wanted to hire a director with a more prestigious résumé. She was seeking a way to let you go. And so, in freeing you both, I am freeing myself. These Gardens, the creation of the man I loved, will be open to the public, and appreciated by it long after I leave this planet. My doctors have not given me much reason to want to linger. It was time for all of us to go on.

"You will soon get formal notification about the contents of my will. Rest assured that the Gardens will be well taken care of, Ethan. The Events Center can go forward, and I have established an endowment that will keep you from worrying too much about the bills from month to month. (But I know you have too much sense to waste my money on hiring Armando Ramos, who has gotten despicably chummy with me lately. I hear he has also been disparaging you. I admit to one red herring. I buried one of his articles in the leaf litter under the eukes. He just annoyed me one too many times).

"Liz has provided well for you, Myron. Ethan, there is something for you in my will, but I am most concerned about being fair to Javier and Maria. Myron, I was not happy that you tried to implicate Javier in my designs. That was not worthy of you. I never thought about the fact that those tiles could be blamed on Javier and Maria. She is a far better artist than I am, as you can all testify, having seen my amateurish mosaics. Javier is not my son, but Alan loved him well. I hope that my money can help them buy a very nice home where they can garden, have sleepovers with their grandkids, and enjoy retirement. Or whatever else they want to do!

"I want to say something about Alan. He would have believed in climate change. He probably would have believed it was human-caused. He wouldn't have cared a fig about keeping that big green lawn. He would be awfully proud of being the city's showcase for green building. He kept up with environmental issues. You and Liz never really saw that about him, Myron. And he came to dislike eucalyptus because they were wind hazards, even before his gardens were open to the public. Sometimes doing something to honor somebody means changing things in the way they might have changed them, had they lived long enough to learn the most current knowledge.

"You may have figured the rest of this out by now. I used to be quite handy in trees, in my youth; I'm far too old to be climbing up in eucalypts now. I did have an accomplice, of sorts."

"It *was* Pedro," Bea said. "I thought so. She couldn't have climbed up in that tree." Ethan raised an eyebrow at her and continued reading.

"My fine gardener Pedro couldn't bear being away from his family any longer. His mother was ill in Mexico, and his little girl was in a car accident. He wanted to go back, but there were no jobs in his town, which is why he'd left his family in the first place. He was afraid for their safety if they tried to cross the border with a coyote, and afraid they'd just be deported if they actually made it. I gave him enough money to set himself up in business in his town, if he'd saw the eucalyptus branch for me. I told him it was part of a play we'd be having at Shandley. And it was. I think perhaps Bea figured out that he helped me. I did pull down the sawed branch; it wasn't too hard to do. Liz was distracted by my horrid art piece, so she never saw me.

"As for that raggedy girl who delivered the roses, she did nothing illegal, although heaven knows what she'll use the money for. I had her cut the roses from Pedro's garden."

"I called Liz on a burner phone the morning of the retreat. I told her exactly where to walk, and I told her what direction to look. You will both be surprised that I have heard of burner phones, but I read mysteries of all kinds, before I created this one.

"I had a bit of fun dropping floral hints about why Liz had died. I hope that you will excuse these as the games of a silly old woman. You know I love puzzles. If either of you were to look in my jewelry case, you'd see a red rose pin, just like the one Liz wore in my mosaic portrait of her. Alan gave it to me, on a particularly beautiful sunset horseback ride. I have a painting in my house that reminds me of it. Of course, Alan knew the language of flowers as well as anyone. Liz stole my love, and yes, I was jealous, which is why I gave her the yellow rose between her teeth. There was a period in her life when she dressed like a cowgirl, as I portrayed her. That was the time of our youth, when I still had hope that Alan might leave her.

"Liz was old, like me. She might easily have lived another ten years. So yes, I played God; I decided that my sons deserved ten years free from the bonds Liz placed on them. Many people will not forgive me, but it doesn't matter now.

"Please tell Bea that I overdid it when I left the yellow roses on her doorstep. Yellow for jealousy. I'm rather jealous of her as a young mother, but the dead roses also meant the end to my jealousy of Liz. I thought Bea would be the most likely one to figure all this out, but I realize I must have terrified her, which was never intended. Clearly, I am losing my grasp of reality. The pain is seeping over far too much of my mind.

"Live well, my sons.

"Mother"

EPILOGUE

There were sunflowers on Bea's doorstep, from a florist. They had to be from Frank. But the card said, "I can play this flower game, too. Sunflowers mean 'appreciation.' It's good to work together again. Marcia."

Inside there was a voicemail waiting for Bea. It was Pat. "I saw the news. You certainly picked a bizarre bunch of characters to work with. But thank God the kids are safe!"

There always had to be a little dig. But for the first time, Bea didn't care. She called Frank and told him about Buffy's farewell letter, and even before she asked him, he promised that this story would not make it into anything he was writing.

"Well, Bea, it looks like your theories weren't crazy at all," he said.

"Why don't you come over tonight to celebrate? After our little staff party at Shandley. I'll call you when I get home." She dropped her eyes for a minute. She could invite him to the party, but she wasn't quite ready for that. His response was a relief.

"Great! I'll bring some good beer."

"Thanks. Yeah, Angus says most of the Queen of the Nights are supposed to bloom! You can't know until the 'day of' if they're going to pop. I probably should be sending email alerts to members to come to a special event, but that's going to have to wait for another year. I want to celebrate tonight with the people my ex calls a 'bizarre bunch of characters.'"

As soon as Bea pulled into the Gardens parking lot, Jessie ran to Angus, who was already in the cactus garden photographing the slowly unfurling petals. Angus let her take the photograph he was framing. Just then, Javier walked up with Maria. They all stayed for a couple of hours as the huge white flowers loosened their layers of petals, floating an intense perfume. Andy was mesmerized and kept saying what he thought the flowers smelled like. "Honey. No, roses. No, milk and honey with cinnamon." Jessie was ignoring the flowers and playing a game with some sticks and pebbles, but she didn't want to go home to bed. She wanted to bring the tent and camp out, but her mother told her they'd have to camp another time.

Maria pulled some *biscochitos* out of her bag to have with a glass of milk before bed, but warned, "Javier will eat them all if you don't take advantage of this offer and head home now."

"That was just an excuse, Mom," said Andy knowingly on the way to the car. He glanced over at his sister, as if to say, "But Jessie fell for it." It was a relief to worry about normal sibling rivalry, instead of the danger of some homicidal maniac getting close to her children. *Not that the murderer turned out to be a homicidal maniac. R.I.P., Buffy.*

It took two bedtime stories and three lullabies to calm the kids enough to go to sleep. Bea tiptoed out, dug her phone out from under a pile of children's books, and called Frank. He got to her house in record time with a six-pack of fine local IPA.

They sank onto the sofa. "The media thinks they have a great story: *Tucson Socialite Kills Friend of Seventy Years Over Old Love Affair, Then Kills Self.* They don't know the half of it," said Frank.

"Thank God. It will be so good to be able to get back to work without worrying if my colleagues and board members are going to knife me in the back. Literally or figuratively."

"So, you've lost Buffy from the board, and Liz, and you're about to lose Myron, right? He's headed east, freed by his mother, as she hoped. The whole old guard will be gone. That leaves Alicia Vargas and Armando Ramos. That's not much of a board."

"No, the by-laws say we are supposed to have three to

nine members. Of course, Armando wants to be a paid staff member, but I seriously doubt Ethan's going to advertise for that research position Armando wants. And it doesn't look like Armando's scheme to depose Ethan is going anywhere, either. So, things are catching up with Armando. Maybe Catalina will see him for who he is, too."

"I know you'd like that."

"Yes. But as far as the board goes... I'm guessing Ethan and Alicia will get some fine folks to join now that they don't have to live in the founder's shadow. And then we'll see what happens with Armando. I have to admit I thought for a while that he was the killer, probably because I don't much like him."

Frank laughed.

"Okay," she said, "I can't stand him. It just shows how biased I can be. I thought he wanted to off Liz so that Shandley would get a big endowment. And he'd get a job doing whatever he felt like doing."

"*I* didn't much care for Myron, the only time I met him, so I suspected him. The guy with the obvious motive. But you know, I just keep thinking about Alan Shandley."

"Alan? That's one person I didn't worry about. He was reliably dead when this whole mess started."

"When it started for *you.* But think about it. He married out of necessity, because Liz was pregnant, and he stayed married his whole long life, despite being in love with another woman. That's not so uncommon, I guess, especially for people trying to maintain an image. Plus, he seemed to have connected with his lover at certain points. But to keep up the charade that Myron was a random adoptee, and not his biological son, sired with his mistress... that would take some doing. Unless he and Liz had some agreement about *that.* As you pointed out, poor Myron, either way they played it. They didn't play it straight, that's clear. And then Buffy never said if Alan knew that Ethan was his son, right?"

"Oh. I guess not. So now we'll never know."

"So, if he knew, or suspected, that's another layer of complexity to Alan's life. And then he apparently thought of Javier as his son. Three sons of one sort or another, but none of them traditional father-son relationships. Too complicated for me. I definitely do not envy him."

"Frank, you're really not thinking of writing a book about this, are you?"

"No. I'd rather spend some real time with certain characters in this story."

"I'll toast to that."

Acknowledgments

Authors often begin their acknowledgments by marveling at how many people have helped them, and they are right.

First, I want to thank Geoff Habiger, the editor/publisher at Artemesia Publishing, who thought Bea Rivers should get a shot. He has been unfailingly patient, helpful, and knowledgeable while leading me through the process of publishing my first book.

Then I'd like to thank Bill Singleton, who has designed an absolutely extraordinary cover. I said I'd like it to be "arresting, botanically correct, with a hint of menace," and he took on the job and delivered beautifully.

Many smart and lovely people have read various drafts and parts of the book. My husband Phil Hastings read the most, and helped in lots of ways, technical and otherwise. Liz Trupin-Pulli provided invaluable feedback and counseling. I am so fortunate to have her professional advice. Betty Spence had the good grace to read it twice, and her editing skills were and are impressive. My little writing group in San Diego—Margaret Harmon, Bette Pegas, and the late and ever-gracious Sara Jones—reviewed the individual chapters. Carolyn Niethammer, Karen Reichhardt, Anne McEnany and Sam Schramski read and commented on the manuscript thoroughly, and some members of my Silver City book group—Ann Hedlund, Susie Coe Brown, Sue Teller-Marshall, and the late Sonnie Sussillo—provided important feedback. Natalie Gore and I had a couple of enjoyable lunches when she helped me with law enforcement issues, and Jim Heard helped with these, as well. Michelle Conklin, the Director of the Tucson Botanical Gardens, gave both encouragement and photographs.

I'd like to thank the late Tony Edland for being Tony and providing the impetus to create Angus McFee.

Most of all, I thank all of the staff members, board members, and volunteers of botanical gardens whom I've worked with over the years. We all share the desire to connect the public with the magic of plants and nature. We've had our disagreements, but fortunately, none have led to murder.

About the Author

Marty Eberhardt directed botanical gardens in Tucson and San Diego and spent many years as a nonprofit staff member, board member and consultant. She now delights in using the right side of her brain to write fiction and poetry. *DEATH IN A DESERT GARDEN* is her first novel. Marty has published several poems and prose pieces, in *The Wilderness House Literary Review*, *The Dragon Poet Review*, *The San Diego Writers INK 2017 Anthology*, *The Twisted Vine Literary Review*, four volumes of *The Guilded Pen*, and *The Silver City Quarterly Review*. She divides her time between the small mountain town of Silver City, NM, and the sprawling beach city of San Diego, enjoying the flora and fauna of both. She lives with her husband, Phil Hastings, and their dog, and spends as much time as possible with her children and grandchildren.